"I should be angry with you, you know."

"I know," Sara Beth said, averting her gaze. "But you're not, are you? Not really."

There was no way Taylor could overlook the sweetness of her smile or the blush on her fair cheeks. Her hair had become mussed during her ordeal and the loose curls made her look like an endearing moppet. "No," he said. "I'm not."

Her grin spread and her greenish eyes twinkled mischievously. "Good. I'd be terribly sad if you were."

"Sad enough to behave and stay safely away from the city center for a while?"

"Well…" Her soft drawl and the way she was gazing into his eyes made him melt inside like butter on a summer's day. "Don't look so worried. I promise I shall behave as well as is sensible."

"That's what worries me," he quipped. When she reached up and gently caressed his cheek, his knees nearly buckled….

Books by Valerie Hansen

Love Inspired Historical

Frontier Courtship
Wilderness Courtship
High Plains Bride
*The Doctor's
   Newfound Family*

Love Inspired

*Second Chances
*Love One Another
*Blessings of the Heart
*Samantha's Gift
*Everlasting Love
The Hamilton Heir
*A Treasure of the Heart
Healing the Boss's Heart

Love Inspired Suspense

*Out of the Depths
Deadly Payoff
*Shadow of Turning
Hidden in the Wall
*Nowhere to Run
No Alibi
My Deadly Valentine
   "Dangerous Admirer"

*Serenity, Arkansas

VALERIE HANSEN

was thirty when she awoke to the presence of the Lord in her life and turned to Jesus. In the years that followed she worked with young children, both in church and secular environments. She also raised a family of her own and played foster mother to a wide assortment of furred and feathered critters.

Married to her high school sweetheart since age seventeen, she now lives in an old farmhouse she and her husband renovated with their own hands. She loves to hike the wooded hills behind the house and reflect on the marvelous turn her life has taken. Not only is she privileged to reside among the loving, accepting folks in the breathtakingly beautiful Ozark mountains of Arkansas, she also gets to share her personal faith by telling the stories of her heart for all of Steeple Hill's Love Inspired lines.

Life doesn't get much better than that!

VALERIE HANSEN

The Doctor's Newfound Family

Steeple
Hill®

Published by Steeple Hill Books™

STEEPLE HILL BOOKS

Steeple
Hill®

Recycling programs
for this product may
not exist in your area.

ISBN-13: 978-0-373-82837-1

THE DOCTOR'S NEWFOUND FAMILY

Copyright © 2010 by Valerie Whisenand

Printed in U.S.A.

A righteous man may have many troubles,
but the Lord delivers him from them all.
—*Psalms* 34:19

To my editor, Melissa Endlich, who believed in me enough to let me branch out and live a vicarious life in the old West, as well as get into plenty of "trouble" in the present.

Prologue

"A righteous man may have many troubles,
but the Lord delivers him from them all."

—*Psalms* 34:19

San Francisco, 1856

Chilling, midnight fog from the bay swirled around
the two men standing together in the narrow alley
bordering Meigg's wharf. The taller one was clad in
the tailored suit, coat and top hat typical of a wealthy
merchant or banker while the other, shivering and
nervously rubbing his own arms, wore the canvas
pants, homespun shirt and cap of a dock worker.

The man in the tall beaver hat scratched a lucifer
and lit his cigar with it, then slowly blew out a

stream of smoke that was quickly lost in the mist. When he finally spoke, his tone was smooth and assured. "You understand what has to be done?"

"Yes, sir, Mr...."

"Shut up. No names. And if anyone asks, you and I have never met. Is that clear?"

"Yes, sir." The workman chafed his calloused hands together to warm them. "When do you want me to do it?"

"In a few more days. I'll get word to you when my plans are firm. Spend your evenings right here in old Abe Warner's so you're ready and waiting when the time comes. Just see that you stay sober enough to hit what you're aiming at. There'll be no further payment if you miss him and shoot me instead."

"I won't miss, mister. I know when to keep away from John Barleycorn."

"Glad to hear it."

"How will I know for sure which fella to shoot? I mean, won't he be dressed just like you?"

"Probably. I'll lure him down here to meet with me after dark, then light my cigar the way I did tonight. When I step back out of the way, kill him."

"How'll I see so's I don't make a mistake? What if there's more fog, like now? The new gaslights ain't workin' hardly anywhere in the city."

The elegant gentleman laughed quietly, menacingly. "I know that, you cretin. Who do you think arranged for the Board of Supervisors to stop paying those exorbitant gas bills? I want it dark, especially around here."

"You've got this all figured out, haven't you?"

"Yes. As long as you do as you've been told, all my troubles will soon be over."

Chapter One

Something was terribly wrong.

Sara Beth awoke with a start. The darkness seemed filled with unnamed dread. She sat up in bed and strained to discern what had disturbed her usually peaceful slumber. At first she thought that perhaps there had been another minor earthquake, which were common in the city by the bay, but she felt no tremors. She did, however, hear plenty.

Downstairs, Mama's voice was raised, pleading, and although Sara Beth couldn't quite make out her stepfather's words, she could hear the rumble of his gruff-sounding reply. That was very unsettling. Mama had married Robert Reese when Sara Beth was but five years old, and in nearly thirteen years she had almost never heard her parents argue.

Rising, she wrapped a shawl around her shoulders over her long nightdress, tossed her head to free her heavy, reddish braid, and tiptoed to the adjoining room to check on her younger half-brothers.

Peeking in at the small beds, she noted that all three boys appeared to be sound asleep. Josiah was the youngest and the most restless. As long as he wasn't stirring, there was a good chance none of the boys had been disturbed.

She gently eased the door to their room closed, went to the head of the stairs and paused at the banister to listen carefully. What she overheard made the fine hairs on the back of her neck prickle.

"Don't go, Robert," her mother pleaded. "Please. For the sake of the children, if not for me."

"You don't understand, Isabelle. I work with the man. I owe it to him to give him a chance to explain before I take my findings to the authorities."

"He's evil. I can see that even if you can't. How do you think he got so wealthy while we scrape by and live so meagerly?"

"Do you wish you'd married him instead? Is that it?"

"No. Of course not."

"Then stop acting as though you want to protect him."

"It's *you* I want to protect, not him. Can't you see that?"

Sara Beth crept silently down the stairway until she reached a vantage point where she could see both her parents. Mama was still dressed, as was Papa. It looked as if they had never gone to bed.

Jerking his arm from his wife's grasp, Robert Reese grabbed his top hat and greatcoat and stormed through the front door, not even glancing in Sara Beth's direction as he passed.

As soon as he had slammed his way out, she hurried the rest of the way down the stairway to comfort her mother. "What's happened, Mama? What's wrong?"

Isabelle covered her face with her hands and began to lament. "I've buried one husband. Now I fear I shall have to bury another."

"Oh, Mama! Papa Robert will be fine. I know he will. We'll pray for him."

Sniffling and wiping furiously at her eyes, Isabelle shook her head. "No, he will not be fine. Not unless I can talk some sense into him before he goes too far." She cast around the cozy room, her eyes alight in the glow from the kerosene lamps, then moved quickly to her sewing table and took her reticule from the drawer. "You mind the boys."

Sara Beth's sense of foreboding deepened. She

reached to restrain her mother, but was shaken off like a pesky insect. The older woman grabbed a hooded cape, threw it over her shoulders and strode purposefully toward the door.

"Mama. Wait. Where are you going?"

"Meigg's wharf. If I don't return by morning, go next door to Turner's store as soon as they open and ask them to send someone to fetch Sheriff Scannell."

"Why do you have to leave us?" Sara Beth asked, the quiver in her voice mirroring the trembling of her body.

"Because there's evil in this old world," her mother said. "And your father is determined to stand alone against it in spite of everything. I have to be by his side whether he wants me there or not." She paused at the open door, her expression somber. "If anything should happen to me, go to Ella McNeil at the Ladies' Protection and Relief Society. She'll take care of you just as she took care of both of us when you were a little girl."

The last thing Isabelle said before she closed the door behind her was, "I love you, dear heart. Always remember that."

Sara Beth didn't even consider returning to her room or trying to sleep. She paced. She prayed.

She fretted. Then she pulled herself together with a final, "Please God, help us," and decided she must act.

She had no doubt that it would be foolish to venture out on foot at night, especially down toward the wharf, although her mother had done exactly that. She also knew that the fate of her entire family might rest on her being there to render aid. That was why Mama had gone after Papa Robert, wasn't it? How could she do less?

It wasn't as though Sara Beth had never been to Meigg's wharf before. She knew the old man who ran the menagerie off the alley down by Francisco Street. Abe Warner had been friendly to her and the boys every time Mama had taken them there to see all his amazing animals. And he'd always let them feed peanuts to the monkeys that roamed free in his watering hole dubbed the Cobweb Palace.

That establishment was run-down and dirty even without all the resident spiders that he refused to kill, but the old man was jolly and Mama had deemed him harmless. If Sara Beth could reach that section of the wharf safely she knew she'd find sanctuary.

The trouble was, she couldn't run off and leave her little brothers alone. Therefore, the first thing she had to do was rouse them and see that they were warmly dressed.

Lucas, the eleven-year-old, would help if she could manage to awaken him sufficiently. And Mathias was pretty self-reliant for being only seven. If they couldn't manage to dress two-year-old Josiah properly, she'd tend to his needs herself.

Rushing up the stairs, she barged into the boys' bedroom, raised her coal-oil lamp high and shouted, "Everyone up. We're going on an adventure and we have to leave right away."

The shot echoed through the rickety frame buildings and resounded along the docks.

An elderly, balding man in his nightshirt stuck his head out the window of his bedroom on the second floor of his establishment and squinted down through the fog, seeking the source of the noise.

Directly below, a woman screamed. Another shot was fired. Then another.

The old man ducked back inside, fumbled into his trousers, tucked in his nightshirt and stuck his bare feet into run-down boots as he pulled his braces over his shoulders. He didn't know what had happened but he'd bet his bottom dollar that somebody was in need of a doctor. And he knew just where to find a good one. He only hoped that whoever had been injured could hold on long enough for proper help to arrive.

* * *

By the time Sara Beth got her brothers ready to go and led them out onto the street, the fog was lifting and there was a pale pink glow beginning to warm the springtime sky just over the hills to the east.

She had hoped to be able to tuck Mama's little single-shot pistol into her pocket for protection, but when she'd gone to fetch it, it was missing, which was comforting because it was probably with her mother.

Sara Beth would be armed only with her wits, her courage and the "full armor of God" that the Bible spoke of. That would be sufficient. It had to be.

At the last minute she'd taken one of Mama's bone knitting needles and had stuffed it up the narrow sleeve of her coat. It wasn't much defense, considering the riffraff they might encounter, but it gave her courage a slight boost.

"Luke and Mathias, you tend to Josiah," she said as she led them down the front porch steps and onto the street. "Take turns carrying him if you must. Just keep up with me, stay very close and don't say a word, you hear?"

Luke obeyed as expected. Mathias was his usual ornery self. "Why?" he asked in a shrill whine. "Where's Mama? And why do we have to go out in the dark? Papa will be mad."

"If you must know, we're going to meet Mama

and Papa." Sara Beth used her most commanding tone to add, "Do as I say or I'll tell them you misbehaved and you'll get a whipping."

Mathias made a sour face and scrunched up his freckled nose, but he fell into step as instructed. Sara Beth turned away so he wouldn't see her start to smile. There was a lot of her own orneriness in her little brother, and his antics often reminded her of herself. Luke was the serious one. Josiah was the inquisitive imp. But Mathias and she were kindred souls, never satisfied to bide their time and always questioning authority.

"I hope and pray I'm doing the right thing this time," Sara Beth whispered to herself as she led the way along the plank walkway toward the Pacific shore. "I truly do."

In the misty light of approaching dawn, she could see a few figures moving silently in and out of the deep shadows. Their presence gave her a start until she realized that none seemed the least interested in her or her little band of children. That was just as well, she reasoned, marching ahead boldly to allay her own fears, because until she reached the safety of the Cobweb Palace she was more vulnerable than she'd ever been.

The shortest distance to Meigg's wharf was via Francisco Street, so that was the route she chose.

Feral cats, busy raiding the rotting garbage dumped at the edges of the raised walkway, hissed and spat as she and the boys passed.

Time and again, Sara Beth glanced over her shoulder to make certain her little brothers were staying close as instructed.

The moist, damp air blowing ashore from the bay seemed to press in on her, its cloying smells almost overpowering. Never before had she noticed how filthy this neighborhood was. Nor had she anticipated how desolate it would seem at this time of the morning.

Always before when she had been there, the area had been bustling with all sorts of people, men and women, rich and poor, intent on their own business or simply out seeing the more colorful sights of the city. To find the neighborhood so apparently abandoned was unsettling.

Suppressing a shiver, she boldly marched on. They were almost there. Her breathing became shallow with anticipation, her heart pounding even more rapidly.

There were lights shining from the windows of the Cobweb Palace when she rounded the final corner. Moreover, many of the local inhabitants who had been out of sight during her approach had apparently been congregating in front of Mr.

Warner's menagerie building. The crowd there was considerable, and it was growing.

Sara Beth paused a moment to assess the situation, then gathered her brothers to her, relieving the older ones of baby Josiah.

"Keep close to me," she ordered. "Grab a handful of my skirt and don't you dare let go until I say so, understand? This crowd is very big and I can't hold all your hands at the same time. We mustn't get separated."

"Yes, ma'am," Luke said, his brown eyes wide.

Mathias, too, nodded, although Sara Beth could tell he'd be off in a jiffy if one of Abe Warner's tame monkeys scampered up and wanted to play tag. Reinforcing her command she glared at him. "You, too, Mathias. Promise?"

He made a silly face. "Okay."

"Good. Now come with me. I think I see Mr. Warner in the doorway of his store and I want him to watch you while I find out what's happened."

She didn't voice all that she was thinking, partly because she didn't want to frighten the boys, and partly because she wasn't ready to accept that her parents might be at the center of the knot of men gathered on the rough, weathered walkway.

The moment Abe spotted her, he hurried over. "You children shouldn't be here."

"I had to come," Sara Beth said, handing the still-sleepy Josiah to the trusted old man. "Is it…?"

"Come inside," he said. "There's no need for you young'uns to see all that. No need at all. No sirree."

Sara Beth grasped his coat sleeve and stopped him. "Tell me. Please?"

She saw him look to the boys, then shake his head. The sadness and empathy in his expression told her more than any words could have. Much more than she wanted to know.

Biting her lip and fighting dizziness, she passed all her brothers into Abe's care, then whirled and ran back into the street, pushing her way through the gaggle of onlookers.

A young, dark-haired man in a black frock coat was crouched down next to three bodies that lay on the walkway. Two had already been covered and he was laying the muddy folds of a wool cape over the face and upper torso of the third to mask it.

Sara Beth immediately recognized the fabric of her mother's skirt and gave a little shriek.

The hatless man quickly stood, focused his dark, somber gaze on her and grasped her arms to stop her from proceeding.

She tried to lunge past him toward the bodies as she fought to free herself. "No. Let me go!"

"I'm sorry," he said, holding her fast. "I did all I could. By the time I got here they were gone to Glory."

"No. That can't be true."

"Unfortunately, I'm quite certain it is," he answered. "I'm a doctor."

"But you're wrong! You have to be wrong."

"I am sorry, miss."

Truth and sympathy were evident in the man's darkly serious gaze.

Bright lights sparkled in Sara Beth's field of vision. Her head spun and she felt wobbly the way she sometimes did during an earthquake.

Her mouth was dry, prickly. She took several shuddering breaths and blinked rapidly, trying to clear her thoughts, to accept what her heart insisted was impossible. It was no use.

Darkness akin to a starless night began to close in on her. She sensed herself descending into a bottomless pit of hopelessness and despair.

No longer wanting to see or hear anything that was transpiring around her, she closed her eyes and let go of a reality too painful to acknowledge.

She was only vaguely aware of someone's strong arms catching her as she sank blissfully into the welcome void of unconsciousness.

Chapter Two

Dr. Taylor Hayward's boots clumped up the creaky wooden steps as he carried the unconscious young woman into Warner's Cobweb Palace.

He laid her atop the bar rather than lower her onto the dusty floor. Hopefully, she wouldn't be offended when she awoke to find herself the center of interest in the old saloon. In his opinion the bar was the cleanest area in the entire building and therefore the best choice as a makeshift fainting couch.

He didn't think the girl was ill or would be in need of his services once she regained consciousness. She had simply received a shock when she had stumbled upon the grisly scene and would surely come around soon without medical intervention.

Still, he planned to stay close to her until she was in possession of her full faculties and to offer smelling salts if need be.

Suddenly, there was a high-pitched shout and a sharp pain in his ankle. He looked down to see a reddish-haired boy of about eight drawing back to give his shin another whack. Before the child had a chance to kick him again, Taylor lifted him by the back of his coat collar and held him at arm's length.

"Whoa, son. Take it easy."

The wiry boy wriggled and swung his fists in the man's direction even though his arms were far too short to reach his intended victim. "What'd you do to my sister?" he screeched.

"This young lady? Nothing. She fainted and I caught her so she wouldn't fall and hurt herself. That's all. What's your name?"

Still struggling and obviously intent on doing more bodily harm, the boy ignored the question. Looking past him, Taylor saw a slightly older child holding a toddler and standing next to the proprietor. Since none of the children was familiar to him, he called out, "Hey, Abe. Do you know this little rascal who's tryin' to take me apart?"

The old man nodded as he laid a hand on Luke's head and stroked his hair. "Aye. That's Mathias

Reese, Miss Sara Beth's brother. So are these young gentlemen. This is Luke and the baby's Josiah."

"Then suppose you tell them I'm an innocent doctor, not a mugger?"

Mathias started to relax but his eyes looked suspiciously moist. "You're a doctor?"

Taylor lowered him carefully to the floor at his feet and released him before crouching to speak with him on his level. "That's right. And it's a good thing, too, because I think my ankle will need medical attention."

The child glanced out the door to where the crowd was still milling around the recently deceased threesome. "Can you fix my mama?"

Taylor's breath caught. Ah, so *that* was why the girl had fainted. Little wonder. She and the boys were apparently part of a family that had just been devastated in a matter of minutes.

He laid a hand of consolation on the boy's thin shoulder before he said, "I'm sorry, son. I got here too late to help her."

"Papa?" Mathias whispered. His lower lip was trembling and he was clearly fighting to keep from weeping.

Instead of answering, Taylor swept the grieving child up in his arms and motioned to Abe to join him rather than leave the unconscious girl unattended.

"Both their parents?" Taylor asked quietly aside.

The old man nodded again. "Afraid so. I don't know what these poor little tykes'll do now."

"What about the other man. Who was he?"

"Can't say. I think I've seen him around but I never did catch his name. He's one of the regular dock workers is all I know. I didn't see everything that happened but I do know that Mrs. Reese managed to shoot their attacker before she fell, too."

"I suppose it was a robbery gone terribly wrong," the doctor said. "What I don't understand is why a refined couple like that was out wandering this neighborhood at night."

Behind him, the girl stirred and moaned. Taylor passed Mathias to Abe Warner and grasped her delicate hand. As her eyes fluttered open, he was struck by the flecks of golden color in her beautiful, green gaze.

She blinked, managed to focus, and tried immediately to sit up.

Taylor gently restrained her. "Lie still. You've had a bad shock and you need a few more moments to gather your wits before you try to stand."

Her eyes widened, misted. "Mama and Papa are both gone, aren't they?"

Taylor knew better than to lie to her. "Yes. I'm afraid so. Are you the eldest of their children?"

She continued to stare at the ceiling of the dimly lit room and act as if she hadn't comprehended.

"Miss?" Taylor chafed her wrist in his hands to help revive her. "Miss? Can you hear me?"

He saw her gather herself, mentally, before she answered, "Yes," and again endeavored to rise. This time he assisted her and carefully helped her down from the bar. She seemed steadier on her feet than he'd expected, so he released her.

To his surprise, she squared her shoulders, lifted her chin and addressed him boldly. "Thank you for your efforts on behalf of my parents, Doctor. I left home in a rush and neglected my reticule but perhaps my father's purse contains enough to satisfy your fee." She paused briefly then added, "Unless he has been robbed."

"Do you think that's what led to this?"

"Of course," she replied, yet there was something odd in her expression. Something that alerted the doctor to the possibility that she was hiding something.

"Would you like me to help you make final arrangements?" Taylor asked.

"Thank you, but that won't be necessary," Sara Beth answered. "I'm sure Mr. Warner can assist me."

"Well, please accept my condolences. If there is

anything I can do for you in the future, feel free to call upon me. My office is located at the corner of California and Montgomery streets, above the Wells Fargo & Co. office." He withdrew a card from his vest pocket and presented it to her. "My name is Taylor Hayward."

For a brief moment, he thought she might refuse to take the card. Then, she pocketed it without comment.

The doctor turned to Abe Warner. "Can you handle everything in here for now?"

"We'll be fine." The apple-cheeked old man gave a wistful smile. "If I can manage my mischievous monkeys and all the birds and other critters in here, a few little boys won't cause me no trouble."

Taylor hoped Abe was right. He had an unsettled feeling about leaving the children in the elderly man's care, yet it looked as if their sister was old enough and wise enough to eventually provide a stable home for them.

She was an extraordinary young woman, he mused. Her fortitude in the face of disaster was not only unusual, it was inspiring. Most women he had encountered, of any age, were flighty and prone to getting the vapors over the littlest fright or disappointment. Miss Sara Beth Reese had fainted, yes, but for good reason. And she had quickly pulled herself together and regained her sensibilities in a way that truly amazed him.

Polite society required that he keep his distance unless summoned, of course, but he would nevertheless try to stay abreast of the little family's circumstances. Taylor had had the benefit of the support of both his parents all his life and he couldn't imagine how he'd have managed without his father's wise counsel and his mother's tempering gentleness and abiding Christian faith.

He glanced back at the Reese children as he stepped outside. They had gathered around their big sister and were clinging to her as if she were the only lifeline from a sinking ship. He hoped—and prayed—that that was not so. There were many opportunities in San Francisco these days, but there were also many pitfalls and dangers, especially for a young, pretty woman with no family elders to advise and cosset her.

As Sara Beth comforted the boys and dried their eyes, she wondered why she, too, was not weeping. She wanted to cry but the tears would not come. Perhaps that was because she still could not force herself to believe her mama and papa were gone forever. Oh, she believed in heaven. That wasn't the problem. Her question was how a benevolent

Heavenly Father could have allowed her and the boys to be left so alone.

"I shall need to return home soon," she told Abe Warner. "Will you escort us?"

"I'd be obliged," he said, "but I can't leave my store with all these goings-on outside. There'll be the law to deal with and then—"

"Will you then arrange for a proper funeral?" Sara Beth asked. "I wouldn't know how to begin."

"Of course, of course. Your pastor should be notified, too. What church do you attend?"

"First Congregational," she said. "At least, Mama and I went and took the boys. Papa never seemed to have the time. He was always working."

"That reminds me," Abe said, frowning. "You'll need to make sure that that workshop of his is secure. Lock it up good and tight, if you know what I mean. There'll have to be an accounting and you wouldn't want to come up short."

"I don't know a thing about that, either," Sara Beth said. "Papa brought the gold dust samples home and assayed them all by himself. None of us were permitted to even watch from outside a window. What shall I do?"

"Leave everything just as it sits," Abe advised. "Whoever assigned him to do the assay work will surely contact you and make further arrangements."

He shook his head pensively. "Always did seem a mite reckless to me, trusting outsiders to handle the dust—even a little of it. Then again, they say there wasn't room for the entire operation under one roof at the mint yet, and your papa was an honest man. He'd had that job ever since Moffat and Company sold to Curtis and Ward, hadn't he?"

"I—I think so." She rubbed her temples. "I'm sorry, Mr. Warner. I can't seem to concentrate at the moment."

"It's the shock, I reckon. You're right about needin' to get on home and take it easy. I'll arrange for someone to drive you."

"No, no. We can walk. I don't have the price of a private hack and I don't know when I'd be able to repay you."

"There's someone close by who has his own buggy. Never you fear. He won't charge a penny."

"But—"

"No argument, girl. I think he's still outside. I'll go talk to him and be back in two shakes of a lamb's tail."

Mathias tugged on her skirt to get her attention. "Are we goin' home, Sara Beth?"

"Yes, dear. As soon as we can."

"What about…?" His lower lip began to quiver as he gazed out the open door.

"Mr. Warner will take care of things for us here," she said, realizing that her real problems were only just beginning. "We need to get on home. I'll fix some nice pancakes. You'll feel better after you eat."

Although she knew that it now fell to her to hold the family together, she had absolutely no idea how she was going to accomplish that feat.

Yes, she knew how to keep house and do the same things her mother had always done, such as sew and prepare meals.

But those were the least of her worries, weren't they? With Papa gone, who would support them? Who would bring in the wages they'd need to survive, let alone flourish as they had been? Sara Beth had had only one serious suitor in the past year and repeatedly rejected his offers of marriage, with her mother's blessing.

Perhaps that was why Mama had specifically mentioned the Ladies' Protection and Relief Society, Sara Beth reminded herself. The benevolent organization had begun as a part of her home church and she already knew many of the members. Mama herself had once worked for some of those dear ladies as a seamstress, until she'd met and married Papa.

Are my skills with needle and thread sufficient to

do the same? she wondered. Was there a chance she might find the kind of gainful employment that had once kept her and her widowed mother off the streets? She prayed so. For if not, she and her brothers were going to be in trouble. And soon.

Abe found the young doctor in the alley, awaiting the arrival of the sheriff. "You bring your buggy, Taylor?"

"Yes. I was just coming in from a call outside town so I already had the horse in harness. I wouldn't have stopped to hitch up otherwise."

"Good. I've got a favor to ask. Miss Sara Beth and her brothers need a ride home. I'd take 'em myself but I don't dare leave my emporium until the furor dies down a bit more. I figure I might as well open the bar and take care of the thirsty curiosity-seekers, too."

The doctor chuckled wryly. "That's what I'd have expected, you old reprobate. Don't you know that rotgut is bad for you?"

"It's a darned sight safer than the water we get from the water wagons," Abe countered. "That stuff's clear green sometimes, especially come summer."

"I can't argue with you there," Taylor replied. "All right. I'll bring my horse around and wait while you fetch the Reese children."

"One of 'em ain't exactly a child, if you get my drift. You okay with that?"

"I'm a doctor," Taylor said. "And we'll have the boys with us as chaperones. As long as Miss Sara Beth doesn't mind riding with me, I'm sure no one else will think twice about it."

The old man snorted cynically. "If you say so. Just keep your interest professional, you hear?"

"Have you taken it upon yourself to look out for the young lady's honor?"

"I wish I could," Abe answered, sobering. "An old codger like me is no good example for those boys, nor a fitting companion for a young woman of Sara Beth's upbringing."

"What do you think she'll do?"

Abe shrugged. "Don't know."

"Does she have grandparents? Aunts and uncles?"

"None, far as I know, although in a case like this folks sometimes crawl out of the woodwork lookin' for a piece of the inheritance."

"Reese had money?"

"I reckon. They live in a pretty nice two-story house over on Pike. You'll see when you drive 'em home. Ol' Robert worked for the mint for a couple of years before he and another fella went into the assay business for themselves."

"Then that's good, right?"

"I ain't sure. Robert used to take lots of samples home with him. It was his job to double-check the official assay and he didn't like to work with a lot of other people watching. All I can see is trouble ahead."

"How so?"

"Can't say for certain. It just seems to me that if anybody was to take a notion to help himself to some of that gold dust, now's the time he'd prob'ly do it. Fetch the buggy. I'll go get your passengers."

Taylor mulled over the old man's opinions and concerns as he led his horse and compact rig into the alley. He supposed he should be thankful for the opportunity to help the orphaned children, but he had to admit that there was more to his interest than mere altruism.

Something about the lost look in Miss Sara Beth's eyes had touched him deeply, irrevocably. In an instant he had come to care about her far more than the circumstances called for. True, she was strong-willed, but she also reminded him of a lost sheep being circled by a pack of ravenous wolves. Given what Abe knew about the whole situation, it was little wonder the elderly man felt a fatherly bent toward the girl.

Taylor huffed and shook his head as his conscience kicked him in the gut. His personal feelings were far from paternal in regard to the lovely young woman. Her hair was the rich colors of autumn, spun into silk. And her eyes were jade gems, sparkling with the very flecks of gold her father had once tested. It was improper of him to notice such things, yet he had.

His outward behavior, of course, would always remain above reproach. He would never stoop to taking advantage of a woman, especially not one as innocent and needy as Miss Reese. He would, however, be more vigilant on her behalf than he would any of his other patients.

Taylor could already tell it was not going to be enough to simply check on her well-being via others. He was going to take a personal interest in the situation. There was no getting around it, no talking himself out of it.

As far as he was concerned, divine providence had placed him in this city on this night and had led him to make these particular acquaintances. It was therefore his duty to do all he could to help—with no thought of gain.

He had not become a doctor in order to get rich; he had chosen his profession because he truly wanted to benefit mankind. If he had wanted a more lucrative career, he would have followed in his father's footsteps and become a lawyer, or in his grandfather's as a judge.

Instead, he had studied medicine for nearly a year under the best minds at Massachusetts General Hospital, then had apprenticed for a while before he'd bid his family goodbye and headed west to practice.

More than half the time he wasn't remunerated for his efforts, and if he was, payment was likely to be a sack of potatoes or mealy flour or an occasional scrawny chicken. He had thought, with the discovery of gold and San Francisco's burgeoning economy, he'd easily find plenty of wealthy patients. Instead, he'd encountered more poverty and need than he'd imagined possible.

That was why he'd begun to donate his services at places like the city's two major orphan asylums and had been so adamant in his insistence that San Francisco needed a care facility devoted solely to the illnesses of children. As it stood now, the poor little things who could not be tended at home were carted off to the city and county hospitals, where they were then exposed to all sorts of nasty diseases and were in the constant presence of morbidity.

His horse nickered, disturbing his musings. Taylor looked up to see the approach of his passengers. He tipped his bowler to them. "Are you ready to go?"

Spine straight, shoulders squared beneath her fitted woolen coat, Sara Beth nodded. "Yes. Thank you, Dr. Hayward. If you will assist me, then hand me Josiah, I would be much obliged."

It worried Taylor to see her so apparently in control of her emotions. The boys seemed a bit sniffly, as children were wont to be anyway, but there wasn't a sign of tears in their sister's eyes.

As he offered his hand, he felt a strange hardness press into his palm. Pausing, he turned her hand over and saw what looked like the end of a smooth, thin stick. His puzzled glance caused her to falter ever so slightly.

"Oh. Forgive me," Sara Beth said, withdrawing the needle and displaying it for him with a trembling hand. "As I was leaving home I thought I might need some method of protection so I brought along one of Mother's knitting needles. I had forgotten about it until now."

"I hardly consider a sliver of bone a suitable defensive weapon," Taylor said. "You could have been hurt walking these streets alone at night."

He saw her countenance darken, her expression close. "Yes," she said, taking the baby and settling him in her lap where she could hold him close. "I might have been shot and killed, mightn't I?"

Without further comment he lifted the older boys

into the crowded buggy, squeezed himself onto the single seat and took up the reins.

Perhaps he had overstepped propriety in his concern for the young woman, Taylor reasoned, but someone had to tell her she had behaved in a most foolish manner. If that decision to follow her parents into the dangers of the night was typical behavior, she wasn't nearly as mature and level-headed as he'd first thought. Nor was she likely to be able to properly care for what remained of her family by herself.

Chapter Three

The steady, rhythmic echo of the horse's hooves on the cobblestone and brick-paved streets provided a soothing tempo until they had proceeded far enough from the busiest areas of the city to encounter hard-packed dirt dotted with muddy potholes.

To Sara Beth's relief, all the younger children had nodded off before the doctor's buggy had reached the portion of Pike Street where their home stood.

"This is it," she said, stifling a sigh and pointing. "That two-story, gray clapboard with the double porches. You can let us off in front."

As the doctor climbed down to hitch his horse to a cast-iron ring, he paused. Tensing, he held up his hand to stop her instead of continuing around to help her disembark. "Wait. Stay there."

"Why? What's wrong?"

"I think I see someone on your porch."

"That's silly. There can't be. Why would anyone…?" Peering at the house, she realized he was right. There was someone on her front porch. And another man on the upstairs porch that mirrored the structure at ground level. Judging by their shadowy forms, both men were carrying rifles.

Sara Beth remained in the buggy as she cupped her hands around her mouth and called out, "Who are you? What do you want?"

The gunman on the lower porch stepped off and started along the boarded walkway toward her. There was no mistaking the menace in his movements. She might have assumed she was overreacting but the buggy horse also seemed nervous, almost unseating her when it suddenly lurched backward to the end of its tether and stamped its hooves.

The man paused halfway to the street and struck a stalwart pose, his boots planted solidly apart, his rifle spanning his chest. "This house is off-limits," he said. "Sheriff's orders."

"But that's impossible. I live here," Sara Beth insisted.

"Not any more you don't. This property is sealed. No one can come or go," the guard replied.

"That's ridiculous. My father, Robert Reese, is the owner." The gunman's cynical chuckle chilled her to the bone.

"That's what you think, little lady. I have it on good authority that this property belongs to the U.S. government now."

"Who told you that? Who sent you?"

"I get my orders from Sheriff Scannell, like I said."

Sara Beth was not about to concede defeat. "Where did he get that authority?"

"From Judge Norton, I reckon."

The doctor had gotten back into his buggy and was again taking up the reins when Sara Beth noticed him. "What are you doing? I'm not going anywhere. This is my home and I intend to claim it."

"Over their objection?" he asked. "I think that would be more than unwise, miss. I think it would be suicide."

"I'm not afraid of them, even if you are."

"Very noble, I'm sure. However, I have only a pistol and you are armed with a knitting needle. How do you propose we overwhelm at least two men with rifles and sidearms?"

"I don't know." Her voice rose. "They're in the wrong. We can't simply give in to such unfairness."

"We can retreat to fight another day," he said. "Hang on." He gave the lines a snap and the horse took off smartly, pushing Sara Beth back against the padded seat in spite of her efforts to lean forward.

She bit her lower lip and fought a swelling feeling of exasperation and powerlessness. This couldn't be happening! Everything she and her family owned was locked up in that house. She didn't even have a hairbrush or a change of clothing for herself or for the boys.

The doctor slowed the horse's pace when they were several blocks away. "Where to?" he asked.

"What?" She blinked rapidly to quell her tears of frustration.

"I can't very well take you home with me and I don't think the Cobweb Palace is a fit place, either. Do you have friends or family you could stay with until we get this mess sorted out?"

She noted his use of the pronoun "we," but chose to ignore the implication. "I have no family in San Francisco and Mother's friends are mostly affiliated with the Ladies' Protection and Relief Society."

Sighing, she said, "I had hoped to delay this decision, but I suppose I have no choice. We shall have to go straight to their orphan asylum. Do you know where it's located?"

She was relieved when he told her that he did.

However, when he added, "I've had the sad duty of treating some of those poor little ones," her spirits plummeted. She and her brothers were now on a totally different social stratum, weren't they? In a matter of hours they had gone from being part of a middle-class family to being destitute, just like the dirty street urchins who begged along the piers and alleys down by the wharf.

Raising her chin and closing her eyes, Sara Beth vowed that as long as she had breath in her body, her remaining family would never have to beg. She would work somewhere, do something that generated an honest living, no matter how meager, God willing.

And, please Lord, show me how to get our house and belongings back, too, she prayed silently. She didn't know how she'd manage to accomplish that, but she would not give up trying, no matter what.

There was no need to hurry the horse along once they were in the clear, Taylor concluded. It was nearly morning. Although the city would soon be bustling with its usual daytime activities, there was probably at least an hour more before the keepers of the orphanage would rise and begin to prepare the first meal of the day.

Mulling over the plight of his passengers made

him so angry he could barely contain his ire. It was fraud and abuses of the law such as these that had brought about the formation of the Vigilance Committee in the first place. The ballot boxes had been rigged, the honest votes nullified by internal corruption and the offices such as judge and sheriff sold to the highest bidders. Little wonder someone in power had had no trouble getting quick control of the Reese home and laboratory.

His own father and grandfather would have been astounded to hear of the despotism rampant in the city. Reform was urgently needed. And as far as he was concerned, men like him were charged, by their own innate sense of honor, to rise up and facilitate a change.

That was why he had joined the Vigilance Committee and why he was still an active member of the widespread secret society. He might not have been able to help Miss Sara Beth immediately, but he *would* help her. Someone was going to pay for turning her and her little brothers out into the night. He was going to see to it.

The horse ambled along the Montgomery block of hotels and up Sacramento Street past the four-story brick Rail Road House, a hotel that boasted accommodations for up to two hundred persons at one time, clean bedding and fresh water. The little figure of a locomotive atop its weather vane was said to anticipate San Francisco's eventual joining with the rest of the States by rail.

Taylor glanced at Sara Beth as he guided his horse up California Street and onto the sweeping, tree-lined drive that led to the orphanage. The building had been, and still was, a palatial private home, although living quarters for the host family were separate from the housing for the orphans and live-in staff. Ella McNeil, the matron, watched over her charges and managed the house with an iron hand. Unlike the Reese children, many of the other orphans had been living on the streets, unsupervised, for months or even years and were therefore in dire need of discipline and moral guidance.

"Miss?" Taylor said quietly. "We're here."

Sara Beth opened her eyes and nodded. "I know. I haven't been asleep."

"Would you like me to come in with you?"

"Yes, if you don't mind. I can manage Josiah, but I can't carry them all. And the older boys may be upset when they realize where we are."

"I understand."

He climbed down and circled the buggy to assist her.

She passed him Josiah, then gently woke Mathias and Luke. "We need to get out here, boys."

Mathias rubbed his fists over his eyes and yawned. "Are we home?"

"Not exactly," Sara Beth said. "We'll be staying here for a bit while we get Papa's affairs settled."

Luke leaned past him to look. "What are we doing here? Where are we?"

"I wanna go home," Mathias began to wail.

"Give him to me," the doctor said. "I'll handle him. You, too, Luke." He held out his arms and took the boys from her one at a time, setting all but Josiah on the ground at his feet and offering Sara Beth his free hand.

When she placed her smaller, icy fingers in his, he felt an unexpected pang of pity. That would never do. A proud woman like her would surely take offense if she even suspected that he was feeling sorry for her.

She faltered once with a little stumble, causing him to reach to cup her elbow.

"I'm fine, thank you. I can manage," she said, righting herself and marching proudly up to the ornate front door of the stone-walled mansion. She rapped with the brass knocker and waited.

When the door swung open and the matron saw her, she greeted her with open arms. "Oh, darlin', I heard what happened. It's awful. Plum awful. You come right in and make yourself at home. We're proud to have you."

As Taylor watched, the stalwart young woman became a child again. Catching back a sob, she fell into Mrs. McNeil's ample embrace. Taylor could see her shoulders shaking with silent weeping as the older woman patted her on the back. He didn't want her to suffer, but he knew that the sooner she began to properly grieve her enormous loss, the sooner she'd recover.

"Let's take the boys in and get them settled," he suggested as soon as the two women stepped apart.

Ella wiped her eyes with the corner of her starched, white apron. "Land sakes, yes. I'm forgettin' my manners. You come along, now," she said to Luke and Mathias. "We've got gobs of other boys for you two to meet and a bunk you can share." She glanced at Josiah in the doctor's arms. "Do you think the littlest one will be all right in there or shall we send him to stay with the infants?"

Before Taylor could reply, Sara Beth snatched up the baby and shook her head. Her tears were gone except for slight dampness on her cheeks. "Josiah stays with me. I won't have him put with strangers."

"Of course, of course." The matron rubbed the girl's shoulder through her coat. "It's been a long, trying night for all of you. We'll talk more about making permanent arrangements later."

No one had to tell Taylor what Sara Beth's

reaction to that would be. He knew she'd resist before she opened her mouth.

"There's no need. We won't be staying. As soon as I get my father's business affairs settled I'll be going back home," she said flatly. "I did want to discuss possible employment for myself, though. Mother's needlework was finer than mine, of course, but she was my teacher and I promise to do my very best. Is there a chance I could work for you like Mother once did, Mrs. McNeil?"

Taylor could see that the matron was hesitant. He privately caught her eye and gave a silent, secret nod.

To his relief, she said, "I'm sure we can find something. Perhaps part-time in the kitchen. Would that suit?"

"Anything will do," Sara Beth said. "If you will show me where to place Josiah while he naps, I can start immediately."

"Nonsense," Ella said. "There'll be plenty of time for that. First, we need to get all of you settled and then fed. When you've rested, we'll talk further."

Sara Beth's deep sigh as a result was almost a shudder. "Thank you. I am weary. And there is so much on my mind right now I can hardly think."

"Little wonder," the doctor offered. "It's been a

long night for all of us. Will you be all right if I take my leave?"

Whirling, she acted surprised that he was still there. "Of course. And thank you for looking after us."

"My pleasure," he said with a slight bow. He touched the brim of his bowler and smiled at the matron, too. "Ladies. If you'll excuse me?"

He managed to retain the smile until he had turned away and walked back outside. There was a deeply troubling wrong to right and no time to waste. If Abe Warner had been correct in his assumption about the gold samples kept in Reese's private assay office, it might already be too late to preserve their integrity.

Nevertheless, he had to try. And his first stop was going to be the Coleman house. William T. Coleman was the president of the Vigilance Committee, and although their roster was kept by number rather than by name, most of the members knew whose loyalty could be counted on in an emergency.

Taylor mounted his buggy and shouted to the horse as he snapped the reins. There was no time to waste. A helpless family was being mistreated and he was not going to stand idly by and watch it happen.

* * *

The middle-aged gentleman arrived on Pike Street in a cabriolet pulled by a matched pair of sorrel geldings and driven by a hireling in a frock coat and top hat.

As he disembarked in front of the two-story frame house, he grinned. This plan had come together even better than he'd anticipated. With Isabelle dead, too, there was no one left to stand in his way, no one who might know what Robert had discovered and thereby ruin his reputation. Or worse.

He strode up the front walk and onto the porch where he was met by the sheriff and two other rough-looking men.

"Sheriff Scannell," the gentleman said with a slight nod. He eyed the others with undisguised loathing and didn't offer to shake anyone's hand, though his own hands were gloved in pearl kidskin to match his cravat. "I see you're keeping company with the usual riffraff."

The sheriff laughed raucously and spit over the porch railing. "Meaning yourself, I suppose, Mr. Bein? You decide yet how you're goin' to explain all this?"

Bein grinned. "As long as the losses are credited to Reese instead of to me, I won't have anything to explain. Harazthy is so engrossed in that new vineyard of his, he barely notices what goes on around the mint."

"What about the Vigilance Committee? Ain't you worried about them?"

"Not in the least. I have it on the personal authority of Governor Johnson that Sherman is about to be made Major General of the second division of militia for San Francisco. He'll soon take care of the vigilantes."

Scannell shrugged and spat again before wiping his mustache with the back of his hand. "All right. If you say so. It's your funeral."

Leering cynically, William Bein snorted approval. "Not my funeral, gentlemen, my partner's, may he rest in peace."

He reached into his pocket and withdrew a handkerchief folded into the shape of a packet and monogrammed with the initials *R.R.* "Take this and see that it's placed in Reese's workshop, Sheriff. Don't make it too obvious, but be sure the gold shavings and dust are still in it when it's found. Do I make myself clear?"

"You think we'd steal from you?"

"In a heartbeat, if you thought you could get away with it," Bein answered. "Only this time you can't. We all need that gold to be discovered in Reese's possession. And since he and Isabelle are both dead, no one will be able to refute the charges against him."

"What about the girl? She came back here."

"What? You didn't let her in, did you?"

"No, sir. We sent her away. She never got out of the buggy."

His eyes narrowed below bushy, graying brows. "What buggy? Reese didn't even own a horse, let alone a rig."

"I think it was that doctor what brought her," Scannell said. "You know. The young one with the shingle on the second floor over the Wells Fargo office."

Bein cursed colorfully. "Oh, I know him, all right. He and Coleman are thick as thieves. He's sure to inform the Vigilance Committee."

"I thought you said you weren't worried about them."

"I'm not. I just don't want any further trouble over this." He glanced sideways at the hired thugs who were still standing guard at the corners of the broad porch. "If need be, we may have to eliminate the girl, too."

"Oh, now, I don't know as I like that idea," the sheriff said, edging away from the well-dressed man. "She's just a young thing. Pretty, too. It's bad enough her mama had to die the way she did."

"Only because she stuck her nose in where it didn't belong," Bein countered. "You lost one of yours in the gunfight, you know."

"I know. But Billy wasn't all that bright to start with. He never should of showed himself when he shot Reese." He was slowly shaking his head as he spoke. "Is it true that the woman got him?"

"That's my understanding," Bein answered. "Which should prove to you that her daughter may be someone to be reckoned with. I don't know about you, but I'm not going to go to jail just because some stupid woman points an accusing finger at me."

"I suppose you're right." Nodding soberly, Scannell perused the broad street. "All right. You look into it and get word to me if you need me to eliminate the girl, too. I won't like it, but I'll see that it's done."

"Good man. And keep your mouth shut about this," he added, eyeing the packet of gold the sheriff was about to deposit in Robert Reese's workroom. "Now, go get rid of that evidence like I told you to."

"What'll you be doing?" the sheriff asked.

"Offering my condolences to my partner's grieving family," Bein said with a self-satisfied smile. "As soon as I find out where the children went, their loving uncle Will is going to offer them a nice settlement and see that they have passage on the next ship back to Massachusetts, where their parents came from."

"You think they'll go? Just like that?"

"When they learn that this house and everything in it has legally passed to me upon the death of their father, I don't see what other choice those little brats will have, do you?"

Chapter Four

The more time Sara Beth spent at the orphanage, the more she remembered about her early life there. Although she had been five when Mama had married Papa Robert, there were familiar smells and noises in that big old house that tugged at her consciousness and made her heart pound.

Friends she had made back then, children she fondly remembered, were, of course, long gone. Those who had come along later and replaced them, however, were so like the ones she recalled that she suddenly pictured herself as very young. And very scared.

Lucas and Mathias had quickly found other boys to interest them and had wandered off to explore the facility, while Josiah had fallen asleep in Sara

Beth's arms. She didn't mind carrying him. Truth to tell, she was loath to even consider putting him down. It was as if she needed the little one's nearness to comfort her, rather than the other way around.

"Let's get you something to eat and a nice cup of hot tea," the matron said, ushering Sara Beth into the expansive kitchen where several other women were already hard at work.

The aroma from the pot of gruel bubbling on the top of the woodstove nearly turned Sara Beth's stomach. That was another of those old, pungent memories, this one best forgotten, she realized with the first whiff. Mama had never prepared that kind of breakfast for any of her family after they'd left the orphans' home, and Sara Beth assumed that memories of being destitute were at the heart of her mother's choices. That certainly made sense.

She blinked in the steamy atmosphere, hoping she was not going to disgrace herself by becoming ill. She knew Mrs. McNeil did her best to stretch the meager rations and was not to be faulted if their palatability suffered as a result. That conclusion, however, did little to relieve her unsettled stomach.

"Ladies, this is Miss Sara Beth Reese, an old friend and former resident," Ella told the other women. They looked up from their labors and she pointed to each in turn. "That's Mrs. Clara Nelson, our cook, and Mattie Coombs, her helper."

Sara Beth managed a wan smile. "How do you do?"

"Fair to middlin'," Clara said with an impish grin, made more amusing by her twinkling blue eyes, apple cheeks and snow-white hair. "You visitin' or stayin'?"

"Visiting. But I do want to make myself useful while I'm here. I'll be glad to help however I can."

Mattie snorted as if in disbelief, turning her thin wiry body back to the stove. Clara welcomed the offer. "You surely can," she said. "As soon as you've eaten a bite you can help me serve the boys while Mattie takes care of the girls."

"Oh, good. My brothers are here, too, and I'd like to look in on them."

Mattie huffed. "I knowed she was stayin'. She's got that look about her. Same as they all get."

Did she? Sara Beth supposed there was a lost quality to her demeanor, although she was not about to openly acknowledge it under the present circumstances. As soon as she had a chance to talk to Mrs. McNeil in private, however, she intended to tell her everything and ask for advice.

The more she pondered the situation, the more she felt there had to be a connection between what she'd overheard her parents discussing and their untimely deaths. Not that their conversation made much sense, even in retrospect.

For one thing, Papa had mentioned someone he worked with in a disparaging manner. The Reese family had treated his partner, William Bein, as part of their intimate circle, including him in social events and even asking the children to call him "Uncle Will." Surely he could not be responsible for anything that had happened.

But there certainly could be other nefarious forces at work, she reasoned. Papa had often expressed disdain for Sheriff Scannell, and that man was proving every bit as disreputable as rumor had painted him. Plus, there was the gold to consider. Anyone who knew that Papa worked for the new mint must also assume he would have samples of gold on hand in his lab. Sara Beth knew many a man had died for riches, especially in the years since 1849.

Reviewing the tragedy, her thoughts drifted to her new benefactor, Dr. Taylor Hayward. His was a difficult profession, one that rarely produced a better cure than most grannies could mix up from their favorite roots and berries. Men like him were an asset to the wounded in wartime, of course, but otherwise might just as well stay in their offices and let the citizenry treat themselves for the ague and such.

Chagrined, she felt empathy for the man. He had obviously attempted to help her parents, and for that effort alone she was grateful. His lack of ability was less his fault than the fact that doctors were little more than hand-holders and tonic dispensers—unless they had served on the battlefield or studied in one of those fancy hospitals back east. At least that was what Papa had always said when he'd gotten sick after spending long, tedious hours in his lab.

Dr. Hayward's presence at the scene of carnage on the wharf had been very comforting, she admitted. But then, so had Abe Warner's, and his calling was not in the healing arts.

Thoughts of the kindly old man brought a slight smile to her face. In a day or so, after she got her thoughts sorted out and decided what course to take, she'd have to walk over to the Cobweb Palace, thank Abe for everything and assure him that he needn't worry.

Taking a deep breath and releasing it as a sigh, Sara Beth realized that she had no certainty that her family would be all right. The way things looked, she would be fortunate to salvage their personal belongings, let alone reclaim the house on Pike

Street. And if Papa Robert's laboratory was not safeguarded, there was no telling how much trouble the mint might cause her.

Surely they wouldn't expect her to be responsible, would they? The sheriff was the one who had moved in and posted guards. Therefore if there were any discrepancies, the explanation for those should lie at Scannell's doorstep.

Only that particular lawman's reputation was built on graft, not honor, according to the talk she'd overheard at church and in her own parlor. His election had been questioned from the beginning, and ballot boxes with false bottoms had been written about in the evening *Bulletin*. Its publisher, Mr. James King, had been crusading against corruption in San Francisco for months and had even withstood threats on his life in order to continue to print the truth.

"That's what I'll do," Sara Beth murmured, elated by her idea. "As soon as I have a chance, I'll pen a letter to the newspaper and ask for information about my parents' murders."

Would Mr. King print such a thing? Oh, yes. He was an honorable gentleman who stood firm against the riffraff and evildoers who lurked among the good people of the city. He would gladly print her missive. And then perhaps she'd see her parents avenged.

Thoughts of allies and admirable men brought Dr. Hayward to mind once again. Not only did he cut a fine figure, there had been benevolence and caring in his gaze. As soon as she was able, she planned to somehow repay his kindnesses. Until then, she would simply take each moment, each hour, each day, one at a time.

To sensibly contemplate the future, when her heart was breaking and her mind awhirl, was more than difficult. It was impossible.

The sun was rising and the city was coming to life as Taylor drove slowly down crowded Sacramento Street and past the What Cheer House. Hotels had proliferated in San Francisco until there were nearly sixty, although none quite as accommodating as the one R. B. Woodward ran, especially if a fellow wanted a warm, clean bath and a decent meal.

Freight wagons and vendors made up the bulk of the traffic to and from the docks. This was not the best time of day to be trying to squeeze a flimsy doctor's buggy through the main streets, wide though they were, so Taylor headed for the livery stable to leave his rig and complete his errands on foot.

There were times, like now, when he almost

wished he were back studying at Massachusetts General Hospital. He had been happiest while learning his trade, always eager to follow successful medical men on their rounds and observe the latest techniques. Everyone agreed that the best teaching hospitals were in Germany but given the state of his purse, such a trip was impossible. Someday, perhaps, he'd manage to travel overseas to study. In the meantime, his place was right here in San Francisco.

"Helping Miss Reese," he added with conviction. He had not been in time to save her parents, but he was going to assist her in every way possible. It was the least he could do.

Leaving his horse and buggy, he made his way along the boarded walk to the Plaza on Portsmouth Square and passed the Hall of Records. As soon as he'd talked to Coleman he'd come back here and see if he could find out who owned the house in which Sara Beth and her family had lived. If, as the sheriff had claimed, it belonged to the government, then he didn't see how she'd ever win it back.

The thought of that sweet, innocent young woman having to take up permanent residence at the orphanage cut him to the quick. Yes, it was well-run. And, yes, it was useful as a temporary shelter. But that was where his approval ended. The place was too cramped, too crowded, and that meant that chances of sickness rose appreciably, especially when summer miasma engulfed the city.

He wasn't sure he believed the experts who claimed that the air itself caused illness, but he did know from experience that the more children who were housed together, the greater the chances that they would catch whatever diseases their companions suffered from. That was a given. And as long as the Reese children and their sister resided with the other orphans, they would be in mortal danger.

The day sped past. Sara Beth saw to it that her brothers were settled in the boys' dormitory and had gone with their fellows to afternoon classes at a nearby school. This new life seemed to suit them a lot better than it did her and Josiah. The little boy had fussed most of the day, wearing her patience thin until she had finally agreed to let him be taken to spend the daylight hours with the other babies under the age of three.

Their parting had brought tears to her eyes, especially when he had begun to sob and reach for her. "No, you need to go with Mrs. McNeil," Sara Beth had said firmly. "Sister has work to do and I can't do it if I'm toting you around." She'd patted his damp cheek in parting. "Be a good boy, now. I'll pick you up after I finish my evening chores. I promise."

Now, up to her elbows in dishwater, she started to yearn for her former life, then stopped herself. "Don't," she said softly. "That's gone. Over. You have to make do. Mama did and you can, too."

"That's the spirit," Clara said as she added more soiled tin plates to the stack by the sink. "Never give up and you'll be much happier. I know I am."

"Have you worked here long?" Sara Beth asked.

"Since my Charlie passed on. Cholera got him right after we arrived. We was goin' to start a little restaurant and get our share of the gold dust the honest way." She sighed, her ample chest rising and falling noticeably with the effort. "I figure at least this way, my skills in the kitchen aren't going to waste."

"I wish I were talented in some special way," Sara Beth said. "Mama had been training me to keep a nice house, just as she did. Beyond that I know very little."

"You can read and write, can't you?"

"Yes. Of course. As a matter of fact, there is a letter I plan to pen as soon as I have a spare moment. Do you know where I can find paper and ink?"

"Ella can give you whatever you need," Clara said with a smile. "I swan, that woman could make a silk purse out of a sow's ear."

"She is amazing, isn't she? I don't know what I'd have done if she hadn't let me stay."

"What about your parents? Are they both gone?"

Sara Beth nodded solemnly. "Yes. I shall have to pay to have them buried and I haven't a cent."

"There's plenty of paupers' graves in Yerba Buena Cemetery. That's where my Charlie is laid to rest. The only thing that bothers me is not having a headstone. Practically no one does, so I guess that makes us all equal, rich and poor."

"I suppose so. Mr. Warner has promised to make the arrangements for me."

"Old Abe Warner? Then let him. He may live like poor folks but that saloon of his has to be rakin' in the gold dust by the bucketful. How'd you come to know him, a fine lady like you?"

That question amused Sara Beth. "Mama loved his menagerie. We used to take our constitutionals down by the waterfront and we'd often stop to feed the monkeys or those beautiful big birds he kept. I even saw a bear there once."

"I reckon he needs all those critters to clean up the garbage. From the looks of his place, he could use a few more, too." She chuckled, then added, "That's better. I know you could smile if you tried."

"I hate to. I mean, it seems wrong, somehow. My family has been decimated and we're in such dire straits we may never recover, yet part of me feels a sense of joy."

"That's the Lord tellin' you He's got the answers," Clara offered. "They may be a while in comin' and may not be the ones you asked for, but He'll look after his children. I've been sure of that ever since I walked through these doors and found my own place of refuge."

"Do you think it's ungrateful of me to wish to leave?" Sara Beth asked.

"No, dear, not at all. Just keep an open mind and heart and listen to God's leading."

"Even when I feel as if I'm spinning in circles?"

"Especially then," the cook said, pausing to give her a motherly hug. "Now, get to washin' them dishes so we can bank the stove and get ready for bed. I don't know about you, but I'm plum tuckered out."

Turning back to the pan of sudsy water, Sara Beth gave silent thanks that Clara was such a wise woman. Now that Mama was gone she'd need friendly counsel like hers and Ella's in order to reform her life, plan her future.

Was it possible to decide anything this soon? she wondered absently. Not really. What she could do, however, was follow through on her idea to contact the *Bulletin* and see if they would champion her cause in regard to her home. They had often taken up the needs of the community and had revealed corruption in city government in spite of threats to their presses and persons. Surely, given this situation, Mr. King would take pity on her plight.

But first he must be properly informed, she added. Her jaw muscles clenched and she nodded to affirm her decision. As soon as she had brought Josiah to her cot in the girls' quarters and had gotten him settled for the night, she would begin to write to the newspaper.

Such a letter would require much thought and careful expression but she was capable. Her penmanship was beautiful and her mind keen. All she'd have to do was make certain she didn't alienate too many important people and yet stated her case in indisputable terms.

Such a goal seemed unattainable, yet Sara Beth was resolute. She could not hope to seize control of her assets by force so she would do it by her wits.

Finishing the dishes, she toted the heavy dishpan to the back door and threw the water onto the steps to clean them, too. At home, she might have tarried long enough to sweep the porch, but not tonight.

Tonight she had a letter to write. A letter that might very well be the most significant missive she had ever composed.

* * *

Taylor Hayward had been disappointed in his earlier meeting with W. T. Coleman. The man had been too secretive to please him and had beat around the bush regarding what the Vigilance Committee might be able to do in respect to the contested Reese holdings.

"That's up to Bein," Coleman had insisted. "He was Reese's partner and as such has control of the assay office."

"Fine. But what about the family home at the same address? Surely we can't allow him to pitch the surviving family members out into the streets."

Coleman's thin shoulders shrugged and he blanched enough that his already pale skin whitened visibly. "It's not that simple. Not anymore. Governor Johnson is talking about putting that general, Sherman, in charge of the militia, and Mayor Van Ness agrees. If they do that, we're in trouble."

"I've never known you to back down from a fair fight," Taylor said.

"I didn't say I was backing down. I'm just telling you that it would be wiser to bide our time. All the newspapers except the *Herald* are already on our side."

"Which is to be expected since James Casey is running it and he's as crooked as they come," the doctor argued. "I'd heard that Casey was thrown out of the Drexel, Sather and Church building by Sherman himself over an editorial so full of lies that even a mule could have recognized its falseness."

"Doesn't matter. We still have to tread softly."

Taylor was beside himself. He paced across the office, then wheeled to face the man he had been counting on for aid. "Suppose there's more to it than what appears on the surface? Suppose Bein is trying to pull a fast one on the government? What then?"

"Then the sheriff should be in charge." Coleman raised his hands, palms out, as if prepared to physically defend himself. "I know, I know. Scannell bought the office for a whole lot more than he'll ever earn legally. That's common knowledge. But it doesn't change anything. We can't wrest control of the whole city from the hands of those criminals unless we're sure of major citizen support. That's all there is to it."

"What will it take to gain that?"

"I don't know," the obviously weary and worried businessman said. "But we can't continue this way for long. When the time is right, we will act, I promise you."

"What if it's too late for the Reese children?"

"That can't be helped." Coleman ran a slim

finger beneath his starched collar as if his cravat were choking him. "I'm not looking forward to the bloodshed that may result."

"Neither am I," Taylor said soberly. "But someone has to do something before we're all slapped in jail or hanged for choosing the side of honor and justice."

"This Reese incident has really gotten you fired up, hasn't it, Doc? How did you get involved in the first place?"

"I was called to minister to the murder victims."

"And you didn't save them. I see. That is unfortunate. But it still doesn't explain why you're so adamant about the real estate."

"There were children left homeless," Taylor said. "I delivered them to the Ladies' Protection and Relief Society. They don't belong there. They belong in the house Scannell is guarding."

"They're better off with Mrs. McNeil. Children couldn't manage alone, anyway."

It was the doctor's turn to loosen his tight collar. "There's—there's an older daughter to look after the little ones," he explained. "She seems quite capable."

"Ah." Coleman smiled. "And pretty, too?"

"That's beside the point."

"On the contrary, that is exactly the point, as I

see it. You have developed some kind of connection to this young, helpless damsel and you're expecting me and my men to assist you in impressing her."

"Nonsense." With a deep, settling breath, Taylor had given up, bid his friend goodbye and left the office building.

In retrospect, he had known denial of his feelings was futile. He did care for Sara Beth Reese. And he could see no good reason for that reaction. There had been and still were, many other comely women in his acquaintance, so why was this one becoming so important to him? Was it her emerald eyes or that long, reddish hair that was so appealing? He had no earthly idea.

Later that day, as he closed his own office and started home to the What Cheer House, where he rented a room, he was still troubled. There had to be more to his burgeoning interest in that young woman and her kin. They had gotten under his skin so quickly it was truly astounding. He supposed Sara Beth's plight, having all those siblings to care for as well as herself, had touched a chord in his heart.

This was not the first time he had found himself caring too much about the welfare of his patients. According to his instructors at Massachusetts General, becoming overly involved in the lives of others was a flaw in his character that he needed to overcome in order to do his job efficiently.

Taylor's real problem, as he saw it, was that he didn't want to lose that touch of compassion that made him who he was. If it interfered with his medical practice, then so be it. He was not about to chastise himself for having feelings for the suffering and downtrodden.

And those poor Reese children were that, and more. For all he knew, they were the victims of the same greed and corruption that already poisoned much of San Francisco politics. If that was the case, they would be fortunate to reclaim anything that had once, by rights, been theirs.

Taylor clenched his fists as he walked, his boots clomping hollowly on the boarded walkway, their thuds lost among the other noises of the still bustling city.

"There has to be something I can do," he murmured in frustration.

Reaching the corner of Montgomery and Merchant streets, he paused, praying silently and then wondering if any of the churches had enough influence to help.

He glanced up and realized where he was standing. That was his answer. The *Bulletin* offices were here. It was the perfect solution. An exposé, written by a man with the solid reputation of James King might force Coleman to call the Vigilance Committee into action. It was certainly worth a try.

A lamp flickered on the second story.

Taylor pushed through the door and took the stairs two at a time.

Chapter Five

Working late by the light of a kerosene lamp in the deserted parlor, Sara Beth labored that first evening and the next to phrase everything just right. Because both paper and ink were dear at the orphans' home, she took special care to make her first draft both concise and perfect.

Satisfied, she folded the sheet of paper several times, addressing the outside of the packet because she lacked an envelope. As soon as her morning chores were completed the next day she'd try to steal away long enough to deliver her written plea. If that wasn't possible, she'd have to entrust it to one of the older boys and hope he carried out her orders correctly.

Rising, she lifted the lamp to light her way back

to the girls' area. When she looked ahead, a tall shadow was falling across the marble-floored entryway.

"Who…who is it?"

"Dr. Hayward."

The breath whooshed out of her and she noticed that she was trembling slightly. "What are you doing here? It must be very late."

"It is," Taylor said, approaching and relieving her of the glass lamp. "I was passing and I saw this light, so I stopped. Why have you not retired with the rest of the staff? Did the latest earthquake bother you?"

"No. I never even felt one happen. It must not have been very strong."

Sara Beth realized she was clutching her letter so tightly she was wrinkling it. Her first instinct was to tell the doctor everything. Then she realized that she really didn't know him, not as a personal friend, at any rate, and should therefore be prudent.

She slid the folded paper into her apron pocket to hide it. "I simply couldn't sleep."

"Would you like me to give you a powder to take? It would relax you."

"No. Thank you." She purposely lifted her chin to emphasize her decisiveness. "You should go. It isn't proper for us to be together like this. I don't

want Mrs. McNeil to think I'm entertaining a gentleman in her absence."

The doctor bowed. "Of course. I'll go. Just let me
see you to your quarters."

Instead, Sara Beth reached for the lamp and
wrested it from his grasp. "That won't be necessary.
I can take care of myself."

"Can you?" Taylor asked. "I wonder."

"What's that supposed to mean?"

"Only that I wish to be of service to you, Miss
Reese. I assure you, I have no ulterior motives." He
fell into step beside her as she started for the hallway.
"I have already tried to assist you in getting your
home back. Unfortunately, the head of the Vigilance
Committee is not willing to act on your behalf."

"I'm not surprised," she replied.

"I was. But I had another idea and stopped by the
newspaper to see if the editor wished to champion
your cause."

That brought her up short. She whirled and held
the lamp high to clearly observe his expression.
"Which editor? Not James Casey, I hope."

"Of course not. He's too involved with Scannell
and the others. I visited the offices of the *Bulletin*."

Sara Beth caught her breath. Was this the answer
to her wish to have her letter safely delivered? It
certainly appeared so.

"Do you know Mr. King?" she asked.

"Very well. And I think he'll print a story about you, if you want. All you have to do is tell him everything and leave the actual preparation of the article up to him."

Thinking, praying and rejoicing, all at the same time, she reached into her pocket and withdrew her letter. "I have already done so. Will you be so kind as to deliver these pages to him and extend my good wishes for his continued success? Papa didn't believe what was printed in any paper but his, and I have high hopes that that loyalty was not misplaced."

"It was not. And your trust in me is not, either," Taylor said soberly. He took the letter and slipped it into his inside coat pocket before touching the brim of his bowler and making a slight bow. "Good night, Miss Reese."

"Good night, Doctor. Will you try to find time to let me know how my words are received? I have done my best to explain my family's situation."

"I'm sure you have. I'll take this to King's home tonight and leave it with him. Tomorrow is my day to check the wards here so you will see me again then."

"I look forward to it," Sara Beth said, struggling to hold the lamp steady and nearly succeeding. She had just placed the fates of herself and her siblings into the hands of a man she barely knew. If he delivered the letter to the editor, all would be well.

If, however, he chose to place it in the wrong hands, she could find herself in true jeopardy. There was only one way to find out and that would not happen until the publication of the story in the *Bulletin,* which would be tomorrow night at the earliest.

Until then, she would hope and pray and try to stay too busy to fret. If the doctor was not as forthright as he seemed, there was nothing she could do about it. Not now. While he had possession of her letter, he also held her fate in his hands. God willing, he would not betray her.

The nattily dressed gentleman stood back, smoking a thick cigar and leaning on his ebony-and-silver walking stick. Morning fog from the bay was thick and slightly hampered the official search of Robert Reese's workshop. As planned, however, one of the examiners easily located the monogrammed handkerchief containing particles of gold.

Bein stayed out of the furor until it quieted down, then made his way to the sheriff. "I see they have discovered proof that my partner was a thief," he said aside. "Tsk-tsk. How distressing. Once that news gets out, his good name will be tainted forever."

"What a cryin' shame." Scannell chuckled. "So, what do you want me to do now? Shall I relieve my men or have them continue their guard duty?"

"Wait and see what the U.S. Marshal's office decides," Bein said. "A lot depends on whether Harazthy gets scared or not. His smelter has been refining for me on the sly and I don't want to ruin that deal."

"Last I heard he was too caught up in being a grape farmer to care one way or the other."

"True. And definitely to our advantage, Sheriff. As long as things are going so smoothly, I suspect you'll be free to be on your way soon. In the meantime, keep the guards right where they are and wait for my orders." He scowled at the taller man's expression of disgust. "Don't give me that look, not if you value your job. I have plenty of influence with the city council."

"Hey, I was elected, fair and square," Scannell insisted.

"You were elected, all right, but there was nothing fair about it and you know it."

"All right, all right. I get the point." He eyed the men who were carrying out boxes of assaying materials and records and loading them into a spring wagon. "What about the girl? Is she going to behave herself?"

"I'm sure she will. I've already booked passage for all those brats and I'm on my way to the Ladies' Protection Society right now to offer my condolences. Once they're on a boat headed for the east coast, we'll have nothing more to worry about."

"I hope you're right."

Bein laughed. "I'm *always* right."

Sara Beth was peeling potatoes in the kitchen when Clara tapped her on the shoulder. "You have a visitor."

"Who? Where?" Her fondest hope was that Dr. Hayward was bringing her word from the newspaper editor.

"Don't know him," Clara said, "but he looks mighty highfalutin for this place. He's waitin' in the parlor with Mrs. McNeil."

"Oh. All right. Thank you."

She was drying her hands on her apron as she hurried toward the front of the converted mansion. The moment she recognized her visitor her heart rejoiced. She ran to him and she threw her arms around his neck. "Uncle Will!"

He patted her on the back the way a parent would

comfort a weeping child. "There, there, Sara Beth. Don't fret. I've come to take care of you."

"Are we going to get to go home?"

"Yes, dear," William Bein said. He stepped back and reached into his breast pocket to withdraw a stiff packet of papers. "Here are your tickets. I've arranged passage for you and the boys. You sail tomorrow morning."

She stepped back and frowned at him. "Passage? To where? We live here."

"Not anymore, I fear. The U.S. Marshal's office has taken possession of your father's workroom and the rest of the property will revert to me, as his partner, once the particulars have been worked out."

She backed away, aghast. "No! Papa would never have left our home to anyone else."

"Your mother would have inherited, of course, but since she's gone, too, it all comes to me."

When he smiled, Sara Beth noticed that the good humor did not reach his eyes. Suddenly, she was seeing the man in a different light. Gone was her kindly old uncle figure and in his place stood a ruthless businessman. A man who was pretending to be helpful while he banished orphans to goodness-knows-where.

"We will not be leaving San Francisco," she said flatly. "Our rightful home is here and it is here we will stay. The boys are happy and I am employed. We have no need of your charity, Mr. Bein." Nodding, she added, "Good day, sir," then wheeled, gathered her skirts and quickly left the room.

She heard Mrs. McNeil calling after her but *dear old Uncle Will* wasn't saying a word. Little wonder. His offer had not only been unfair, it had been transparent. He wanted their land, for whatever reason, and she and her brothers were standing in the way. Well, too bad. If it took her the rest of her life she was not going to cease trying to find a legal way to reclaim her rightful home. Situated next to Turner's store the way it was, it would make a decent boarding house or even a commercial establishment if she decided to take up dressmaking or millinery.

Truth to tell, she was far from certain that she was in the right in this instance, but something in her nature insisted that she stand firm. There had to be a point at which doing what was just triumphed over the letter of the law.

She tried to think of a scripture that would back up her conclusion and failed, although she did recall plenty about the trials of Job cited in the Old Testament.

Those thoughts and the conclusions they led to made Sara Beth shiver. A lot more could go wrong before the good Lord interceded to bring justice, couldn't it?

Her biggest concern was how she was going to withstand, let alone triumph over, whatever terrible, unknown trials still awaited her.

It was late afternoon on the third day since the murders before Taylor was free to return to the orphanage. He immediately sought out Sara Beth and found her in the kitchen, as expected.

He removed his hat and greeted everyone. "Good day, ladies."

Clara was the first to speak. Grinning, she offered up a plate of freshly baked cookies. "Afternoon, Doctor. I think I have just the thing for whatever ails you."

"Umm. Thank you," Taylor said, returning her smile as he accepted the cookie plate but keeping his gaze fixed on Sara Beth. "I always know just when to arrive, don't I?"

"Pretty much," Clara said. "Looks to me like Miss Sara Beth needs a break. Why don't you two take these cookies into the parlor while I brew you up a pot of tea?"

"You needn't wait on us," Sara Beth said, blushing. "I have no desire for tea but I would like to speak to Dr. Hayward in private."

Taylor stepped aside to give her room to precede him. Instead of going to the parlor, however, she walked out onto the veranda and raised her face to the sun.

He followed. Young children were playing a game of hoops on the lawn while older girls jumped rope to a singsong chant, providing a perfect covering noise for their conversation.

"I delivered your letter to James King," Taylor told her.

She clasped her hands tightly together, her emerald eyes glistening. "What did he say?"

Although Taylor wanted to take her hands and offer physical comfort, he restrained himself. "The article will appear tomorrow. He didn't have time to get it written and set into print for this evening's edition."

"I suppose that will have to do."

"You seem more troubled than the last time we met," the doctor said. "Are your brothers all right?"

"They're fine. Even Josiah. He's the oldest one in the nursery, but he seems happy. And Mathias and Luke are already attending school, although I suspect that Lucas will soon have to find a job to help with our keep. I just hate to see him have to grow up so fast."

"I'll see what I can do to delay that." His brow

knit. There was clearly more to the young woman's disquiet than concern for her brothers' fates. "What else is wrong?"

"How do you know something is wrong?"

"Because of the suffering in your eyes," Taylor said softly. "You don't have to confide in me, but you might feel better if you chose to do so. Have you had to arrange the burials? Is that it?"

She shook her head soberly. "No. Abe sent word that he has taken care of everything already. I saw no reason to expose the boys to more trauma by making them watch the interment, and I didn't think it was fair for me to go without them. I hope that was the right decision."

"Absolutely. Is that all?" He saw her jaw muscles clench and her chin jut forward.

"No. The rest is so unbelievable it's hard to fathom, let alone explain. William Bein, the man my father and mother trusted, has usurped our home and tried to ship us off to who knows where."

"Are you certain?"

"Positive. He showed me the packet of boat tickets he'd bought."

Laying aside his bowler and also placing the plate of cookies atop the broad stone railing that bordered the raised veranda, Taylor gave in to his instincts and grasped her hands. To his relief, she not only allowed his touch, she seemed to welcome it. "All right. Start from the beginning and tell me everything."

"There's not much to tell that I truly understand," Sara Beth said, tightening her grip on his fingers. "He and my father were partners in the assay business. Papa did the laboratory work and Uncle Will—I mean, Mr. Bein—handled the books and the safe transport of the ore."

"That might explain his connection to the workshop, but it should not mean he owns your house, too."

"That was my thought, exactly."

"Perhaps there's a way to convince him to split the two halves of the property."

She shook her head, her eyes misty. "Even if it were that easy, I doubt he'd listen to reason. I spoke with him, looked into his eyes. There is no Christian love in that man. Not a drop. I can't believe how taken in my father was by his perfidy."

Taylor was stroking the backs of her hands with his thumbs, when he realized it was inappropriate and quickly released her; he was stunned by how strongly he yearned to touch those soft hands again. Embarrassed, he cleared his throat. "Then we shall have to wait for the article in the *Bulletin* to create a groundswell of support for your cause. Once Bein realizes that his reputation is at stake, he should be more inclined to listen to reason."

"And if he doesn't?"

"If he doesn't, then I'll have to revisit my friends on the Vigilance Committee."

"Papa always insisted that we shouldn't take the law into our own hands."

"The law in this city is a travesty," Taylor said flatly. He handed the plate of uneaten cookies to her and squared his hat on his head. "I have to check on the health of the children before I leave. Take heart, Miss Reese. The hands of true justice may be slower than you and I would like, but they will triumph."

"I would like to see my brothers," she said. "May I accompany you on your rounds?"

He tipped his hat and offered his arm, delighted when she slipped her small hand into the crook of his elbow. "Please do."

Before they left the porch, Sara Beth handed the cookies to a nearby girl, instructing her to serve them to her playmates and return the plate to the kitchen.

"There. Now I have no good chores to keep me from accompanying you."

"I certainly don't want you to feel that I'm coercing you," the doctor said.

"It's not that." She lifted her hem slightly to step over the threshold. "It's the sadness I feel whenever

I see all those poor, lonely children and realize that my family is now a part of that assembly."

"For the time being," he replied. "You will get your rightful inheritance. I'll see to it."

Her resulting smile and gaze of gratitude warmed his heart until he realized that there was a fair chance that he would fail. San Francisco politics were probably no worse than those anywhere else, but they were far from honest. Factions warred against each other until it was hard to tell who was really in the right. A man could be arrested for little cause, tried and hanged in the space of a day. There were many in power who would look the other way if Bein and his ilk had enough money to pay off the right people to get what they wanted.

Except for Coleman and the others on the secretive Vigilance Committee, there was no one Taylor could trust. No one. And so long as that was true, Taylor had to keep control of his instincts to protect Sara Beth and her brothers. It was one thing to help them now, but when this was over, Sara Beth would find a protector—a husband—who could provide better for her family than Taylor ever could. To help her meant keeping that lovely woman's best interests in mind and forming no attachment that would compromise her future happiness.

Chapter Six

When Sara Beth got her hands on a copy of the *Bulletin* the following afternoon, she was astounded to find her story on the front page. The headline read, "Dastardly Deed! Local Couple Murdered in Cold Blood," and went on to detail her parents' demise.

As she read, she realized that Mr. King had dramatized her tale until it read more like an adventure serial in *Frank Leslie's Illustrated Weekly,* yet the facts remained.

Although reading the entire article made her heart ache, she forced herself to continue until she had taken it all in. Mr. King had not named names, but there was enough innuendo and oblique reference to leave little doubt as to which factions were in the wrong and who may have been responsible.

In truth, his account sounded far more plausible than her plain treatise had. The editor believed them to be neither random killings nor a robbery gone wrong. He inferred that they had been planned and were part of a larger, more sinister plot.

That thought caused Sara Beth's pulse to speed. Could it be so?

In an instant she was certain. Everything was starting to make more sense, especially since Mr. King had learned that her poor father was being blamed for the theft of gold he had been hired to assay.

She was about to crumple the newspaper in disgust when Taylor Hayward walked into the orphanage kitchen. He was clutching a copy of the *Bulletin* in one hand, his medical bag in the other.

"I can't believe this! Papa Robert did not have a crooked bone in his body," she blurted.

"We all know that," Taylor assured her, setting the black bag aside and approaching her. "That was the point James was trying to make when he wrote it that way. Anyone who knew your father will see that there's no truth to the accusations. I'm positive tomorrow's paper will follow up on that conclusion."

"How can anyone believe such lies about my father? And what about the others? Papa wasn't the only one handling that gold. There were smelters and refiners as well as the branch mint. He often said there was too much unexplained loss from the manufacturing of the coins and ingots, but he could never prove theft."

Suddenly she recalled the conversation she'd overheard the night of the murders. In her excitement, she grabbed the doctor's forearm through his coat sleeve. "Wait! I just remembered something else. Papa told Mama he was going to the wharf to meet someone he worked with and give that man a chance to repent. Do you suppose he finally did find proof of theft and was planning to face the person he felt was responsible?"

"Possibly. But who?"

"Who is profiting already? And who was in a position to frame my father for crimes committed by others?"

"William Bein."

"Precisely." Sara Beth began to pace and wave the newspaper for emphasis as she spoke. "I can't let this happen. Robert Reese rescued me and Mama from our struggles and gave us a wonderful home. He was the kindest, most forthright, Christian man I ever knew. I will not stand idly by and let his good name be ruined."

"What do you plan to do?"

"Write to Mr. King again and provide any other details I can recall, no matter how obscure. Now that I see what kind of exposé he plans, I can better tailor my words to fit his model."

"Are you sure that's wise?"

She arched her eyebrows and cocked her head. "Wise or foolish, I shall do it. No one can deter me. Don't even try."

Smiling slightly, Taylor raised his hands in mock surrender. "Far be it from me to stand between an angry woman and her goals." His grin spread. "I'll be glad to deliver any other notes you want to dispatch. In the meantime, would you like to visit the sick ones with me again? Your presence seemed to cheer them a lot yesterday." As he spoke he picked up his small satchel.

She turned to Clara. "Can you and Mattie spare me?"

"Of course, dear. You go with the doctor. We have everything in hand." Although she spoke plainly, there was an extra twinkle in her eyes and a knowing smile on her face that made Sara Beth a bit self-conscious.

Blushing, she left the kitchen. Clara was right, even if she had been teasing a bit. There wasn't enough work in the efficiently run kitchen to keep three women busy all day. Honestly, there was barely enough for two as long as they were both hard workers like Clara and Mattie.

As the doctor led the way down the hall toward the sickrooms at the rear of the mansion, Sara Beth's thoughts were racing. She almost had to run to keep up with his longer strides.

At the door, she grasped his arm to stop him. "Wait! I have an idea."

"All right. What is it?"

"I want to become your assistant. I don't mean a real nurse, just a helper. You know. Someone you can teach how to care for the sick little ones and be trusted to carry out your orders when you can't be here and the others are too busy looking after the healthy children."

His brow furrowed as he stared at her. "Why not become a real nurse? You're certainly intelligent enough."

"Thank you." Unsure of how he had come to that conclusion, Sara Beth waited for him to elaborate.

"I read the letter you wrote to the newspaper," Taylor said, beginning to smile. "It was quite impressive."

"Really?"

"Yes. Really." His grin widened. "On my next visit, I'll bring you some medical books to look at.

Then, if you decide you can cope with all the trials we'll face, you may also become my amanuensis and help me keep proper records."

Her countenance sobered as she began to fully comprehend what he was saying. "The possible loss of life, you mean?"

"Yes. Medicine is not the science it may one day become. We're learning new things all the time. A few years ago, a doctor in Austria proposed that something as simple as hand washing might prevent hospital fever."

Intrigued, Sara Beth hung on his every word. "Really? How?"

"No one knows. Many doubt him, but the man has the statistics to back up his conclusion. I, for one, see no reason not to employ the technique. It certainly can't hurt."

"In that case, I'm thankful this property has its own well. That water the trucks deliver to most of the city is fetid, especially as the days warm in the summer."

"I've been using a diluted chlorine solution," Taylor said. "When a few drops are mixed with any water, everything clears, even odor, though I wouldn't recommend that anyone drink it." He displayed his palm. "It's hard on the skin if you don't wash it off, so it can't be good for the gut. Don't worry. You won't be actually touching any very ill patients, just writing down my findings for me."

"I'll do whatever you say. I want to make myself useful." His warm smile in reply blessed her.

"Then let's start by seeing how our little patients are doing today," Taylor said.

He held the door for her and Sara Beth walked boldly into the sickroom. Dealing with ill children was going to be harder than peeling potatoes or drawing well water to supply the kitchen, but at least here she'd feel needed.

One look at the wan, coughing child in the nearest bed, however, almost caused her to change her mind. Only a sincere desire to help the doctor and the children kept her steps steadfast.

"Have you seen this?" Bein shouted, throwing the crumpled sheets of the *Bulletin* onto James Casey's desk at the office of the *Herald*.

"Calm down, William. He's just stirring the pot. There's nothing he can prove."

"You wouldn't be so complacent if it were you he was slandering."

The younger, thinner man shrugged. "As a matter of fact, one of my spies tells me King is planning to do exactly that."

"You have skeletons in your closet?"

Casey guffawed. "You might say so. I was not always the upright businessman you see before you."

"There are no upright businessmen in this room," Bein countered. "Myself included. And proud of it, if you must know. Besides, you just got elected city supervisor. If he'd had anything on you, he'd surely have revealed it before the election."

"True. But one never knows what unwelcome information may yet surface. I was not exactly a model citizen of New York."

"Just because you spent some time in Sing Sing prison? Nobody's perfect."

"I'll be satisfied as long as we're not run out of town on a rail or tarred and feathered," Casey said, chuckling. "Now get out of here and forget about the *Bulletin*. There's nothing King or any other editor can do to us that we can't handle via my weekly."

"Except that you have to wait until Sunday to rebut."

"All the more time to plan an impressive response," Casey said. He arched a brow and eyed the newspaper his ally had brought in. "How much of that article is true, anyway?"

"All of it," Bein replied with a snide smile. "Why?"

* * *

The pile of books the doctor had delivered to Sara Beth weighed more than all her brothers put together. She had asked him to leave them in the parlor where she could choose one at a time rather than take them to the girls' ward and worry about the children being overly curious. Some of the illustrations had made her blush, but she kept reading, fascinated by her studies. The more she read, the more eager she was to learn, and the more she appreciated and revered her teacher.

When she saw Taylor Hayward the following day she was quick to tell him so. "I can't believe all you have to know," Sara Beth said, eyes wide. "Those medical books are amazing. I had no idea the subject was so complicated."

"You were able to understand the texts?"

"Most of them, yes," she replied, averting her gaze and blushing.

"I do apologize if some of the chapters upset you, Miss Reese. There was no way I could censor them to protect your refined sensibilities. I would have if I could."

She looked up and met his gaze. "I know that. I must admit that there were parts I skimmed rather than read every word. I thought, if it were necessary to know everything, I could always return to those chapters and study them then."

"Very wise." He smiled benevolently. "Truth to tell, most medical men refer to their textbooks often when making a diagnosis. No one could possibly remember every detail well enough to be certain."

Sighing, she, too, smiled. "Oh, thank goodness. I was afraid my poor mind was feeble."

That made Taylor laugh and Sara Beth felt her cheeks growing warmer as a result. "Well, I was," she insisted.

"I totally understand. In medical school I often felt that way."

"You went to a real school? Where?"

"Massachusetts General Hospital. Why do you ask?"

Embarrassed to have doubted him, she explained, "I had thought... I mean...the doctor who used to come by when Mama and I lived here had apprenticed under another man. I'm impressed that you actually attended a medical college."

"That's becoming more and more common these days," Taylor said, "although many practitioners of the healing arts are still given licenses after very little real study."

"Could I... I mean, might I do the same?"

"Become a *doctor?*"

Sara Beth could tell by his expression of astonishment and disbelief that she doubted her abilities and resolve. Nevertheless, she spoke her mind. "Why not? Surely there are many modest women who would rather be treated by someone like me. Someone who understands their reticence to put themselves in a man's hands." She felt her cheeks flame. "Figuratively speaking, of course."

"Of course."

It didn't assuage her embarrassment to see that the doctor was struggling to keep a straight face. She couldn't tell whether he thought her goal was silly or if he was merely amused at her rosy complexion and nervous manner.

Gathering her courage, she straightened and looked him in the eye, refusing to be cowed. "All I ask is that you give my idea some thought. According to the text I read this morning, there are many women who suffer needlessly because of their modesty. That is perfectly understandable, and if I can somehow assist them, I feel it is my duty to do so."

Taylor finally broke into a grin. "Bravo, Miss Reese. I applaud your ambition. But let's start with some simple nursing duties before you try to take over my job. All right?"

She didn't appreciate his laughing at her lofty goals, but she could nevertheless appreciate his opinion. Of course it would be a long time before she was ready to be a real doctor. In the meantime there was plenty to do and even more to learn by observing Dr. Hayward. As long as she applied herself and kept an open mind, she might eventually succeed beyond his or anyone else's wildest imagination.

Was that a foolish aspiration? She didn't think so. Not only did it give her a tangible goal for the future, it helped take her mind off seeking retribution.

She wasn't about to forget what had happened to her family. She simply needed something good to look forward to. Something that would perhaps give her life purpose and redirect her thoughts away from vengeance.

Surely, God was going to even the score, as the Good Book promised. The only question Sara Beth had in that regard was whether or not the Lord was leading her to assist. She was not the kind of person to sit back and let her world spin out of control if she could help it. The first chance she got, she would once again write to Mr. King, as she'd already planned.

What would she say? That answer came easily. She would tell him about William Bein's attempts to send her whole family away. Let the powers that be make of that what they would. She knew it was nothing but a shameful attempt to steal what rightfully belonged to her and her siblings. If *Uncle Will* thought he was going to get away with cheating them out of their inheritance, then he had another think coming.

She shivered, remembering the cold look in Bein's eyes. If she never had to actually meet that man face-to-face again, she would count it a blessing.

A doctor? Taylor was still smiling to himself as he returned to his hotel for the night. Sara Beth was amazing in both her courage and her ambition. He supposed there were female doctors somewhere, although he had never personally met one. The notion was just so farfetched it amused him. He could envision the reactions of some of his stuffy professors if a young, pretty woman like Sara Beth Reese walked into the operating theater and wanted to observe, let alone begin to practice the healing arts on her own.

Entering the imposing What Cheer House, Taylor headed for the formal dining room. This was one of the most prestigious establishments in the city and also provided real baths in the basement, something most other hotels had not yet added to their amenities. Taking rooms there was his one extravagance and one he sincerely hoped he'd be able to afford to continue. It wasn't on par with eastern hotels, but it was one of the best available in San Francisco.

Gas-lighted chandeliers illuminated the separate

dining area off the lobby. Crisp linen cloths draped the small tables, which were graced by only the finest china, silver and crystal goblets. Although no strong spirits were served, the hotel was nevertheless always crowded.

Waiting for a table, Taylor spotted W. T. Coleman, waved to him and was motioned over. He gladly obliged.

"Evening, W.T."

The wiry man offered a chair. "Join me?"

"Delighted. How goes it?"

"The raw oysters on the half-shell are delicious. I highly recommend them."

Taylor huffed and lowered his voice. "I had something other than food in mind when I asked. Any word on the problem you and I were discussing?"

Coleman shook his head, glancing from side to side as if expecting to be accosted any second. "No. And I don't want to discuss it in here. The walls have ears."

Waiting until a black-suited waiter had taken his order and departed, Taylor continued his query, albeit quietly. "Have you seen the latest issue of the *Bulletin?*"

"Yes. Do you think that's wise?"

"What? Printing the truth?" He unfolded his napkin and laid it across his lap.

"No. Letting King quote that girl. Do you have any idea how dangerous that may be for her?"

"I didn't notice any direct quotes," Taylor said, frowning. "Did he actually mention her by name?"

"Not in the article. Since I figured out where most of the information came from, others will, too. Where is she staying now that she has no home?"

"At the Ladies' Protection and Relief Society headquarters. She'll be safe there."

"Only if she keeps her head down and her mouth shut. A few more letters like the last one King printed and anything may happen."

Taken aback, Taylor leaned closer and grabbed his companion's wrist. "What do you mean, *printed?* He was supposed to build a feature on her letter, not run it."

Coleman nodded, looking decidedly uncomfortable. "Well, it's there. On page three. If all you read was the article, you missed the most important part of the paper."

"I'll stop and cancel my dinner order on my way out," Taylor said, standing and throwing his crumpled napkin across his place setting. Sara Beth fully intended to write again, this time making specific references to William Bein. Printing that letter would not only open her to a libel suit; it might endanger her just as W.T. had suggested, especially if she grew impatient and entrusted it to someone else to deliver instead of waiting until she saw him again.

"Where are you bound?"

"To head off a catastrophe, I hope."

"Good luck," his friend said.

"I'll need more than that," the doctor answered in passing. "I'll need divine intervention." He smiled over his shoulder. "Feel free to pray for us."

"Gladly," Coleman said. "Seems like I've done little else of late."

Taylor had also been praying almost constantly for the past week. Even when he didn't consciously realize he was doing it, he was often reminded that his thoughts had brought Sara Beth and her brothers before God.

The way he saw it, he had been put into their lives to guide them through these dark valleys. Yes, he knew it wasn't all up to him, yet he also believed that his wits and his friends would be of use in the long run.

Right now, however, his task was to stop her from having another letter published. If she insisted on writing it, as he assumed she would, he must convince her—and James King—to make the missive anonymous. Otherwise, she would place herself in even worse danger. If that were possible.

Chapter Seven

Sara Beth's immediate concerns were temporarily set aside when she learned that Lucas had been causing trouble. Separating him from the other boys, she led him into the garden after supper.

The breeze off the Pacific was balmy and helped clear the air of the disagreeable odors drifting up the hill from the wharfs. Gulls soared overhead and squawked at each other like argumentative children.

Speaking of which, her brother was acting as if she were imposing upon him by asking him to accompany her outside for a private talk.

"You can't tell me what to do. You're not my mama," the boy grumbled, scuffing his feet on the grass that a few grazing sheep kept manicured.

His attitude cut her to the quick. "Of course I'm

not Mother. No one will ever take her place. But we're family. We have to stick together, especially right now."

"Why? You don't care about us. You put Josiah in the nursery so you can go off with that doctor."

"That's not true. I've been working in the kitchen, too. I have to contribute to our keep. You know that."

"Fine. You can do what you want. I'm not staying here."

She frowned and grabbed his shoulders to force him to look at her instead of staring down at his toes. "Of course you are. We all are. Listen to me, Luke. This place is only temporary. As soon as I can get our house back we'll all go live there, just like we used to. I promise."

"Oh, sure. How are you going to do that?" His face started to show more than anger, as if he were struggling to keep from breaking down and weeping.

Sara Beth tried to embrace him and was rebuffed. Tearing free from her grasp, the eleven-year-old ran across the lawn and disappeared behind a hedge.

Rather than pursue him, she merely stood there, astounded and more than a little hurt. Lucas wasn't the only confused one in her family, was he? She was plenty upset herself, and poor Mathias had been moping around ever since he'd learned he was still expected to attend school. Only Josiah seemed to be content and that was because he didn't understand their dire straits.

Perhaps she should have made more effort to include her older brothers in her activities, she reasoned. If Luke felt needed, then maybe he'd be less likely to balk at every order he was given. There had to be some way to reach him and give him a task that made him feel important.

Of course! Encouraged, she called to him. "Lucas? Would you run an errand for me? I need someone trustworthy to carry a letter downtown."

His tousled head poked out from behind the bush. "Me? I get to go? Alone?"

"Yes," Sara Beth said, trying to sound nonchalant when her stomach was churning and her heart racing. It was only slightly risky for the boy to be out and about this late in the day. If she intended to make him feel useful and a part of their quest, she had to let him participate, even if it did cause her slight concern.

Luke was slowly returning, hesitant but clearly intrigued. "What do I have to do?"

"Carry a letter to the newspaper building on the west side of Montgomery Street. Do you know where that is?"

He nodded. "Uh-huh."

"Good. When you get there, I want you to deliver

my letter to Mr. James King, the editor. Give it to no one else. Understand?" Reaching into her pocket, she retrieved a folded piece of paper and offered it to the boy.

When he reached for it, she kept hold till she'd finished speaking. "This is a very important job, Lucas. For Mama and Papa. You have to follow my instructions precisely and get back here before dark."

"Okay." Grinning, he snatched the letter from her grasp and danced away, gamboling backward on the grass. "Can I have a penny for candy?"

"I don't have any money. I'm sorry. But someday I'll reward you, I promise."

Watching the boy dash off, clearly elated to have a job to do, she hoped she'd made the right choice. If Luke's new attitude was any indication, all would be well.

In her heart, however, she continued to harbor reservations. That boy had always been the quieter brother, but he had a stubborn streak a mile wide. Mathias would have simply joked about running away while Luke truly meant any threat he issued.

Sighing, she let herself drink in the beauty of the placid grounds, the blooming spring flowers, the distant calls of birds and the hum from the city that lay below the mansion on the hill. Under almost any other circumstances she would have been delighted to tarry in such a lovely place.

Now, however, try as she might, she could not seem to find respite from the cares that threatened to burden her beyond bearing. At times of introspection like this, she was always reminded of all she had lost and of how difficult it was going to be to triumph over the current adversity.

"Father," she whispered into the evening air, "what must I do? How can I possibly win?"

The only answer she received was a fleeting sense of peace. That was shattered almost immediately when a familiar buggy raced into the circular driveway and stopped in front of the orphanage.

Taylor Hayward disembarked. There was a frown on his face and his jaw was clenched. Sara Beth's first thought was that Luke had been injured and the doctor was bringing her the bad news.

She hurried to join him. "What is it? What's wrong?"

"Nothing, I hope," Taylor said, taking her hands. "I came to fetch your letter for the newspaper."

"Oh, that." Relieved, she smiled. "Don't worry about a thing. I've already sent it."

"You *what?*"

His outburst took her aback and she pulled away, confused and alarmed. "I—I gave it to my brother

Luke a few minutes ago. He needed to feel useful and I thought—"

"Get in," Taylor ordered. "We have to overtake him before he gets you into worse trouble than you already are."

"I don't understand." She let him assist her into the buggy and watched as he climbed into the driver's seat and grabbed the reins.

"King printed your letter."

"Of course. We knew that."

"No. I don't mean he used the facts you gave him. I mean he printed the whole thing, verbatim. I hadn't noticed it on a back page but it was there, all right, complete with your name at the bottom."

"So? I'm not ashamed of what I said. It was all true."

"Who else was privy to the conversation you heard your parents having?" He glared at her. "Never mind. I know you were the only one. This is as much my fault as it is yours. I should never have left your letter with King without stipulating that he keep your identity a secret."

"That's not sensible," Sara Beth argued. She had to hang on to the end armrest of the padded bench to keep from bouncing around and sliding into him on the corners. "My testimonial was needed to give the story credence."

"Not when you're the only witness who can accuse Bein," Taylor argued. "If something were to happen to you, he'd have no one else to fear."

That notion made her shiver. The doctor was right. As long as she continued to insist on justice and had the newspaper on her side, there was a chance that Bein would decide she was a danger to their plans, whatever they might be. If he and his men were as dishonest as she thought, they could easily decide to resort to more murders.

And right now her defenseless brother was walking the streets of the city, alone and bound for the very place that lay at the seat of the exposé. If anything bad happened to Luke because of her foolish choices, she'd never forgive herself.

Glancing at the stalwart man driving the buggy, she included him in her silent prayers for deliverance. Her heart was filled with gratitude and more. This virtual stranger had come into her life and, in the space of mere days, had become such an integral part of everything it was a wonderment.

Sara Beth knew that the doctor was merely a kind man who would have helped anyone in need. That wasn't the problem. As she saw it, her biggest obstacle was going to be remaining aloof in his presence when what she really wanted to do was throw her arms around him and thank him for his assistance from the bottom of her heart.

She would never be so bold, of course, but she couldn't help wondering if envisioning such an embrace was not as big a sin as actually acting on that desire. She certainly hoped not, because thoughts of being held in his arms refused to go away, no matter how hard she tried to stop entertaining them—especially when he was seated so close.

Taylor thought he spotted Luke trotting along the boardwalk that flanked Montgomery Street. He pointed. "There. Isn't that him?"

"Yes. Hurry!"

A slow-moving freight wagon was in their way. By the time it had passed and the doctor had maneuvered his buggy to the side of the road, the boy had disappeared.

"Where is he?" Sara Beth grabbed Taylor's forearm.

"I don't know. He can't have gotten as far as the *Bulletin* office this quickly."

Taylor jumped down, tied his horse to a hitching ring and circled the buggy to assist his passenger.

"Maybe he ducked into the mercantile," Sara Beth suggested as he lifted her down. "He said he wanted to buy penny candy. I didn't have any money to give him but he might have found some in the street."

Taylor arched his brows, trying to recall exactly who and what had been near the boy in the last moments before he'd vanished. The street had been crowded, as usual, with strolling couples, businessmen heading home and the usual loitering ruffians and lowlifes. Any of those people might have interfered with the boy's progress, although he figured that one of the latter was the most likely. It was even remotely possible that Luke had been shanghaied, although his small size was in his favor. Until he grew taller he wouldn't be useful on shipboard as anything but a cabin boy.

"You go that way and I'll go this," Sara Beth said.

Taylor grabbed her wrist and held tight. "No. We stay together. I don't want to lose you, too." The moment he spoke he knew that such a masterful attitude would not sit well with her. It didn't.

She dug in her heels and resisted, leaning the opposite direction. "Luke is my brother. It's my fault he's here. I'm going to find him."

"There's no time to argue. You're coming with me."

"I'll scream."

"Go ahead. The longer you stand there arguing, the farther away the boy will be." Taylor knew the moment she was ready to capitulate because her eyes grew misty and her shoulders slumped.

Without further discussion, he began to lead her toward the closest mercantile at a hurried pace. His heart was racing and his throat was dry. Their first task had to be locating the boy and making sure he was safe. After that, they'd go to the newspaper office and make certain that no more of Sara Beth's actual letters were printed.

She kept calling Luke's name to no avail. They checked the nearby stores, then proceeded along the street, peering into every doorway and down every alley.

By this time, Taylor had released her wrist and she had placed her slim hand in his, apparently unmindful of how their association might look to bystanders. He was glad, because it not only showed growing trust on her part, it pleased him greatly.

He hoped and prayed he would prove worthy of her confidence. If they didn't locate the missing boy soon, he would have to solicit outside help. Alerting Sheriff Scannell was out of the question, which left only the Vigilance Committee as his other option. He wasn't looking forward to asking W.T. for another favor, but in this case, he'd do whatever it took to succeed.

They *would* succeed, Taylor promised himself. They had to. This poor young woman could not stand to lose another loved one. The notion was unthinkable.

Covering the few blocks between where they had seen Luke and the *Bulletin* office took only minutes. Taylor squeezed Sara Beth's hand to offer moral support before he said, "Here we are. Let's go in and talk to James. Maybe Luke has already been here."

"You go," she said with a deep, telling sigh. "I'll wait out here and watch for Luke."

Taylor could tell she had to make an effort to give him a wan smile.

"Really," she went on when he hesitated. "I'll stand right here while you go see Mr. King."

"You won't leave? You promise?"

She made an *X* on her chest with one finger. "Cross my heart."

"All right. I'll be right back."

It was hard to take his leave. He scaled the stairs leading up to King's office two at a time. He burst through the door, startling his friend, and found himself looking down the barrel of the editor's pistol.

"Whoa!" Taylor raised his hands. "It's just me."

"Sorry. I've been receiving death threats and it

pays to be ready." Stowing the gun in his desk, the editor asked, "What brings you here? You look agitated."

"I am. Have you seen a boy about this high?" He held out his hand. "Miss Reese sent her brother to bring you another letter and we can't locate him."

"No." Frowning, King strode to the window and scanned the street below. "No boy has been here today. What was in the letter?"

"More proof of criminal activity and details about what has happened to the Reese family since we last spoke."

"Does the child know what he's carrying?"

"I doubt it," Taylor replied. "His sister didn't think it risky to send him and he hasn't been gone long. We nearly overtook him until he vanished about a block away. Being only eleven, it's possible he got distracted."

King huffed. "In a city as colorful as this, a grown man might. I'll keep my eye out for him. He may arrive yet."

"If he doesn't, I'm going to need help searching. Can I count on you?"

"Of course. How about the others on the committee? Have you asked them to help?"

"Not yet. I was hoping Luke had been here

already and we'd just missed seeing him." Backing toward the door, Taylor said, "I left Miss Reese keeping watch downstairs. I'd best go back to her."

"You left her there? Alone?"

"Yes." He frowned. "Why not? This is a good neighborhood."

"Normally it is," his friend said. "Trouble is, I can never tell who or what may be lurking out there, just waiting for me to make a mistake."

"You really are scared, aren't you?"

King shrugged and seemed to relax. "Yes and no. The Good Book says we have a certain amount of time allotted. I just don't want to waste mine recovering from a beating. Or worse." He pulled his top hat from a hall tree, donned it and joined Taylor. "Let's go see this girl and settle the problem of her lost brother."

"You're sure you want to come? Don't you have work to do here?"

"It will wait. I have today's paper printing in the basement and nothing pressing at the moment." He smiled. "Besides, if Miss Reese wants to, she can tell me her story in person as we search for the boy."

"All right. But you have to promise you won't print her name the way you did the last time."

"I have to prove my allegations," the editor

argued. "The whole story revolves around her family."

"I know." He led the way down the stairs. "Just be as discreet as you can."

"I am always the soul of discretion, dear boy." King was grinning as he stepped out into the waning sunshine. "Now, where is this young woman with the fantastic story?"

Taylor swiveled right and left. There were plenty of folks jamming the street and boardwalk but there was no sign of Sara Beth Reese. Nor of Luke.

"I left her right here. I swear it." Shading his eyes, he peered into the distance, hoping against hope that he would spot her yellow gingham skirt among the plethora of springlike colors adorning other women.

There was a flash of brightness here and there but nothing definitive enough to spur him to action. Taylor's heart lodged in his throat. She had promised she'd stay put. Only one thing might have drawn her away—the sight of her brother.

Which way? Dear God, where?

Frantic, he grabbed James King's arm. "Her hair is reddish and her eyes are green. The boy's, too, I assume. We left in a hurry so she wasn't wearing her bonnet or shawl."

"All right," the older man said. "Calm down.

We'll find her. Don't worry. It's me the villains are after, not Miss Reese."

Taylor's eyes met his as he said soberly, "I sure hope you're right."

Chapter Eight

Sara Beth was breathless, frightened beyond belief. Not only had she spied Luke, she had seen that he was being held by the wrist and dragged along the opposite side of the street. The boy was struggling to get free, as she would have expected, but he and the surly-looking man who had hold of him were being summarily ignored by the passing gentry. Only the hooligans seemed to be taking notice and all they did was cheer the man's efforts to control the unruly child.

She started to call out, then changed her mind. If she didn't alert anyone to her presence she'd have a better chance of overtaking Luke unobserved. At least she hoped so. What action she might take when she did face her brother's captor was another matter.

Empty-handed and defenseless, she knew she

had only her wits on which to rely. "Such as they are," she murmured, disgusted at herself for leaving the orphanage without so much as her reticule. What on earth was she going to do?

That didn't matter. All that counted was getting her brother back. Lifting her skirts to keep them out of the foul mud as she crossed the street, she began to zigzag around wagons and horses. Luke must not get away again. She would not allow it.

Please, God, please, she whispered to herself. *Help me.*

The closest freight wagon stopped, blocking her path. Sara Beth deftly dodged around the rear of it, barely escaping being run down by a buggy and team headed in the opposite direction. That driver shook his fist and cursed at her. She ignored him. Every effort was focused on Luke and the burly, filthy man who was still holding him hostage.

Closer. She was drawing closer. Just twenty yards more and she'd be able to lay hands on the boy, to wrest him from his captor.

Panicky and frantic, she gasped as a painful stitch in her side nearly doubled her over. She didn't think she had cried out until she saw the man pause, wheel back and stare at her.

Luke spotted her at the same time. "Sara Beth! Help!"

"Let my brother go," she demanded loudly.

The surly, middle-aged man merely chortled and spit into the street.

Sara Beth resorted to the only weapon she had—her voice. Screaming, "Kidnapper!" at the top of her lungs, she screeched so loudly that every person within earshot stopped and stared. "He's kidnapping my brother," she yelled, pointing. "Stop him! Somebody help us. Please."

No one stepped forward. In the intervening seconds of indecisiveness, however, Luke managed to break free. Weeping and wailing, he dashed to Sara Beth and fell into her arms.

She embraced him tightly. When she looked up, expecting an attack, the man had melted into the crowd and disappeared.

Suddenly, all the strength and resolve that had sustained her during her wild pursuit was gone. In its place was overwhelming fatigue. And tears of gratitude.

Cupping Luke's cheeks, she raised his face to hers. "What happened, honey? Tell me."

"He—he just grabbed me for no reason," the boy stuttered.

"Are you sure that was all there was to it?"

"I'm sure," Luke insisted.

"All right." She dashed away her tears and took

his hand. "Come on. We have to get back to the newspaper office. Dr. Hayward will be looking for us."

To her surprise, Luke dragged his feet. "No. I don't wanna go back there."

"Why? Is that where you were taken from?"

He nodded, sniffling. "I—I was just going in the door when somebody grabbed me."

"All right. We'll stand across the street and watch the office from there. We can call to the doctor when he comes out."

"By the mercantile?" Luke asked, his tears all but forgotten.

The quick change in his mood was off-putting. "Yes. Why?"

"'Cause I want some candy."

"I already told you, I don't have any money."

"That's okay," the boy said, reaching into his pocket and fisting a coin. "I do."

Sara Beth drew him to a bench along the walkway and forcibly sat him down. Leaning over so she could stare into his face, she asked, "Where did you get money?"

"I found it."

"Luke, no lies. I want the truth. Who gave you that coin?"

When no answer was forthcoming, she guessed

and saw the truth revealed in her brother's guilty expression. "That bad man gave it to you, didn't he?"

"No. No, I found it on the street."

"What did he want you to do for the money?"

"Just go with him. But I changed my mind. You saw."

A disquieting thought suddenly occurred to her. "Where is my letter, Luke?"

The boy looked away, refusing to meet her inquiring gaze. "I dunno. Maybe I lost it."

"Or you *sold* it," she said, her heart racing and her thoughts awhirl. "That's what really happened, isn't it? Oh, Luke, how could you *do* that?"

"It was just an old letter. Who cares? You can write another one."

"I have never understood the scripture 'Spare the rod and spoil the child' until now," Sara Beth said. "If Papa Robert were here he'd whale you good." She gritted her teeth. "And you'd deserve every lick of it."

"You can't spank me," Luke said defiantly.

"I could, but I won't," she replied. "The damage is already done. If that letter falls into the wrong hands, all of us may be in terrible trouble."

"You can't scare me. I ain't scared of nothing."

"Of anything," she corrected. "You looked pretty frightened to me when that ugly man was hauling you down the street."

"I wasn't scared. Not really."

She shook her head in resignation as she plopped down on the bench beside the boy and sighed. "You may not be afraid, little brother, but personally, I'm terrified."

By the time Taylor spotted Sara Beth and Luke, his patience was more than worn thin, it was nonexistent.

"Where were you?" he demanded before he noticed the tears in her eyes and the distress in her expression.

Instead of answering him she stood, slipped her arms around his waist and stepped into his embrace, totally banishing his righteous anger. Taylor felt her shaking with silent sobs and his heart melted.

He gently patted her upper back through the fabric of her dress. "Take it easy. You're safe now. And I see you found Luke all by yourself."

All she did was nod against his shoulder.

"Then everything is fine, right?"

"No," Sara Beth answered. "It's awful. Luke sold my letter to some stranger."

"What?" Furious, he glared down at the cowering boy. "Who? Who did he sell it to and why?"

"For money, of course." She recovered her composure and stepped away far enough for Taylor to see her face. "The man wasn't satisfied, though. He tried to kidnap Luke, too."

"So that was where you went. I figured it had to be really important to make you break your promise to wait for me." He stared into her emerald gaze. "Do you have any idea how worried I was?"

"Yes. And I'm sorry. I just saw them for an instant and I was afraid if I waited for you to come back it would be too late. Luke would be gone for good."

"That's probably true. What did the man look like?"

Sara Beth shrugged. "Like every dock worker around here. He was big and burly and dirty. And when he leered at me I think I saw some of his front teeth missing, although I can't be positive. I was more concerned about getting him to release Luke."

"Of course. Other details may come to you later, after you've rested and had a chance to think calmly."

With a hand at her back, he gently guided her toward the newspaper office, noting that all he'd had to do was cast one threatening glance at the boy and he'd fallen into line behind them. At this point, that derogatory letter could be in anyone's hands. The thief was likely one of Bein's henchmen, which was all the more reason to worry, Taylor told himself.

"I want you to come back to the *Bulletin* with me and speak to James King. He was helping me search for you and went back inside when I spotted you. These streets have become dangerous for him since he printed your first letter. You can tell him the rest of the story and let him decide how best to proceed. Will you do that?"

Sara Beth nodded. "Yes. Of course. We should also inform Mrs. McNeil of where we are. She's bound to miss us and worry, too."

"I'll send a runner." He frowned at Luke. "A trustworthy one this time."

"He's been through a lot in the past week," said Sara Beth. "I should have explained how important the letter was to us all."

"No," Taylor countered. "He should have done as he was told and not allowed himself to be bribed."

"I just wanted some candy," Luke grumbled. "Mama always bought me candy when we went for a walk."

At that, the child's voice broke and Taylor's heart softened toward him. Even adults made mistakes and at only eleven, the boy had little practical experience on which to draw. He'd learn. He was probably already a lot wiser than he'd been an hour ago.

The question that continued to vex the doctor was who had sent the kidnapper for Luke? Who now possessed Sara Beth's letter, and what might he do after he had read it?

That unspoken question sent a shiver zinging up his spine and prickled the hair on the back of his neck.

Sara Beth perched on the edge of one of the captain's chairs in King's office, her fingers laced together in her lap, her spine stiff. The editor cut an imposing figure with his dark hair and eyes and the beard and mustache that outlined his thin mouth. He had been staring at her and Luke for what seemed like an eternity before he nodded, apparently in agreement with all she and the doctor had revealed.

"I believe I may have discovered a connection between your nemesis and mine," King said. "Casey has been seen in the company of William Bein, not to mention Sheriff Scannell. They make strange bedfellows."

"Agreed," Taylor said, pacing the small office. "The question is, what can any of us do about it?"

"First things first." King smiled over at Sara Beth. "Miss Reese's story will appear next week, without any mention of this interview, although I imagine that whoever was behind the attempted abduction of her brother is probably having this office watched day and night."

"Then they know I'm here." She took a shaky breath.

"Undoubtedly. If they didn't see you enter this time, they have your letter, at the very least. That is unfortunate." Glaring at Luke, King nevertheless refrained from verbal chastisement.

She was not so inclined. "My brother understands that what he did was very wrong. He will not make a similar mistake in the future. What I wonder is how there can be a connection between William Bein and this Mr. Casey? They travel in totally different social circles, don't they?"

Taylor nodded and spoke up. "Yes and no. Both are deeply involved in the politics of the city and both have a monetary stake in how it is run. That alone would make them allies."

"And I have the two of you," she said, standing and beginning to smile. "I would not trade either of you for the whole gang of those horrid men." She offered her hand to the editor and he shook it briefly.

"I plan to live up to your high opinion of me," King said with a slight bow. "And I know Dr. Hayward feels likewise."

Sara Beth didn't have to look over her shoulder to know that Taylor had stepped closer and was now directly behind her. She could feel his presence the same way she felt the rays of the summer sun or the radiant warmth of a hearth in the winter. It was an awareness she had not sought, yet she craved its comfort and the unspoken support she felt every time he drew near.

"We should be getting back to the orphanage," Taylor said softly. "It will be dark soon."

She turned and gave him a most thankful look. "Are you offering Lucas and me a ride in your wonderful buggy?"

"It will be my pleasure." He squared his hat on his head and crooked his arm. "Shall we go?"

Slipping her small hand through the bend of his elbow, Sara Beth felt as if she were being escorted to a fancy dress ball on the arm of a true prince, just like the story of Cinderella. Taylor Hayward was that, and more, to her. If he had not come along and taken such a personal interest in her cause, she didn't know what she would have done. How she would have coped.

Oh, there was Ella McNeil and the other women who supported the work of the Ladies' Protection and Relief Society. But those dear ladies had homes and families of their own to worry about. They could not, should not, be asked to cope with the serious problems that the surviving Reeses were facing. That was a job for the honest men of San Francisco, assuming Mr. King could find any who would stand with him.

Sara Beth knew her cynicism was misplaced. She had listened to enough of her parents' conversations to be certain that there was an underground element ready to insist upon justice. If and when the right time came, they would band together and act on the side of right, no matter what corrupt government officials said. She didn't look forward to vigilante justice but if that was the only kind offered, she would accept it.

Making her way to the waiting buggy, she held tight to Taylor's arm and scanned the crowd that thronged the street and nearby business establishments. Somewhere in that multitude was the man who had tried to steal her brother, and surely he hadn't acted alone. Were they connected to William Bein? Or was that too simplistic a notion?

Shivering in spite of the balmy evening, Sara Beth stumbled and had to lean on the doctor's arm to keep her balance.

He laid his hand over hers where she had grasped his arm. "Are you all right?"

"No," she said honestly, fighting the tears that

brimmed and threatened to slide down her cheeks. "I am far from all right. I feel scared and lost and nearly at the end of my endurance."

"Little wonder."

She saw the doctor cast a disparaging glance at Luke as the boy clambered into the buggy ahead of her and took a seat on the floor, legs crossed.

"It's not just because of what my brother did," she insisted, letting her protector assist her in climbing aboard. "It's everything. I feel as if there are villains lurking everywhere, ready to pounce. It's very disconcerting."

"You'll be safe enough once we get you home and inside those stone walls where you're among friends."

"The orphanage is more like a prison than a home," Sara Beth told him as he joined her and took up the reins. "I know I shouldn't feel that way. Perhaps it seems worse because I dare not leave. If I did, I'd always be jumping at shadows and wondering who is plotting to harm me or my brothers."

"This, too, will pass," Taylor said. "Be patient."

She knew he was right. And wise. And privy to much more inside information than he had chosen to share with her. Still, she was adrift in her current situation because she didn't know enough details about those who stood against her.

Would old Abe Warner know anything useful?

she wondered. She was overdue for a visit with him and there was no time like the present.

"I'd like to swing by the Cobweb Palace on the way home, if you don't mind," Sara Beth said. Before the doctor could object she added, "I owe Mr. Warner for taking care of my parents' final arrangements, and I'd like to make sure everything is in order."

Sighing, the doctor nodded. "All right. It's not far. Just promise me you won't go running off again."

Sara Beth placed a hand on her brother's shoulder and answered, "We will stay together and remain beside you at all times. Won't we, Luke?"

Although he merely mumbled, he did deign to nod so she was satisfied. The boy had to be suffering and confused. Although he did not have to shoulder the full responsibility for everyone else in the family the way she did, he was still to be pitied. They all were.

Which was another reason why she wanted to see Abe. He had gone beyond normal kindness in order to assist her. She wanted him to know how much she appreciated his efforts as well as demonstrate that she was happy and well cared for at present. He was like the grandfather she had never known.

That thought made her smile wistfully. Abe

Warner was not only a colorful character; he was quite unlike the real grandparents her mother had spoken of so fondly. However, since those dear ones had gone to Glory long before Mama and Papa, she had no one else. Her fondness for Abe had grown as she had, with maturity bringing understanding. He was a lonely old man whose animals were his only real family and whose business served as his social circle, such as it was.

She and Mama had both tried to get him to come to church with them, but he had always begged off. That was probably just as well, since he didn't exactly smell like a rose. His heart, however, was as pure as the very gold her father was accused of stealing.

"I will clear your good name, Papa," she whispered. "I will. I swear it."

Beside her, she felt Taylor tense and sensed that he was looking at her so she forced a smile for his sake.

"That's more like it," he said, returning her grin. "I'm glad to see you're feeling better."

Better? Perhaps, she reasoned. Then again, maybe she was merely getting to the point where she could accept what had happened and move forward. There was certainly no option of going back. Her days as the cosseted daughter of a trusted assayer and a member of polite society were over.

Sara Beth, Lucas, Mathias and Josiah Reese were now nothing more than numbers on the books of the Protection Society.

Still, she reminded herself, she should be doubly thankful for Ella's kindness in taking them all in when she and Luke were technically beyond the ages specified in the society's charter. He was a year older than was generally allowed for boys, and she was not at all qualified because she was neither an unwed mother nor a widow with small children to support.

Thank You, Father, that they bent the rules this time, Sara Beth thought, amazed that it had taken her this long to realize how truly blessed she was.

The buggy stopped in the dusky alleyway next to Meigg's wharf. She shivered, remembering the last time she had been there and hating the fact that she'd have to pass the place where the bodies of her poor parents had lain so recently.

Taylor reached over and covered her hand. "Are you sure you want to go through with this? I can take a message to Abe for you instead."

"No. I'm going to go speak with him, to thank him in person. I owe him that, and more."

She watched him climb down, circle the buggy and offer her his assistance. As she placed her hand in his, she was struck once again by his warmth, his gentleness. He had long, tapering fingers, skillful surgeon's fingers, she noted, just as the medical texts had described.

Right now, however, it was not the doctor's medical expertise she was appreciating. It was his caring expression and the slight smile he was bestowing upon her. If she lived a hundred more years she didn't think she'd ever see a kinder look in anyone's eyes.

That thought, and the one that followed, made her falter. Taylor caught her by the waist and lowered her feet carefully to the ground.

"What's wrong?" he asked, frowning.

Sara Beth was not about to tell him what tricks her mind was playing on her. When she had thought of having many years of life ahead of her, her imagination had immediately countered with the notion that this next breath might be her last.

She had wobbled when she had realized how real that possibility might be. The man who had slain Mama and Papa had died, too, but if he had not been working alone the threat of assassination was still there. Still lurking in some black-hearted knave like William Bein who might easily hire another scoundrel to slay her. Or her whole family.

Chapter Nine

The Cobweb Palace was not an establishment Taylor would have chosen for Sara Beth or her impressionable brother to visit, particularly at this time in the evening. Dock workers and others had bellied up to its bar till there was no room for one more man to squeeze in. Raucous laughter echoed from the celebrants enjoying French brandy, Spanish wine or English ale, and the aroma of hot food mingling with that of the old man's menagerie was anything but appetizing.

Sara Beth shrank back in the doorway. "Maybe this was a mistake. I've been here with Mama many times and it was never like this."

"That's probably because you came on a Sunday afternoon. A saloon is a saloon, even if there is enough stuff crammed in here to make it a museum or a zoo."

Spotting the top-hatted old man behind the bar, Taylor motioned him over. As soon as Abe recognized Sara Beth, a grin lifted his whiskered cheeks.

She greeted him tearfully and gave him her hand. He patted it affectionately, sending a twinge of jealousy through Taylor and leaving him shocked by his untoward reaction. The young woman had intimated that she thought of Abe as a grandfatherly figure, so why did his innocent attention to her seem so off-putting? Might he covet the easy affection between the two despite his vow to keep his feelings out of it?

"I—I just wanted to thank you in person," she told Abe, watching as Luke played with a monkey that was chained atop a keg at the rear of the room.

"Nothing to thank me for," he said. "Have you been to the cemetery yet?"

The doctor saw her glance at her brother before she said, "No. I know Mama and Papa are in heaven. There's no need for me to see their earthly resting places."

"Well, I put up a marker for them anyway," Abe told her. "It's just temporary till I can get one carved proper."

"I will repay you, somehow, someday," Sara Beth vowed.

"Ain't no need for that. None at all." He gestured toward the bar. "These fine gentlemen ponied up plenty for the graves and there's enough left over for a nice headstone."

"I thought stone markers weren't allowed at Yerba Buena."

"It ain't that. It's the way the sand hills drift over the graves that hide 'em. But don't you fret, Miss Sara Beth. I'll see to it that the plots are kept clean so you can find 'em when you're ready to go pay your respects."

"Thank you." She leaned close enough to kiss the old man's cheek. "And God bless you."

"He has, He has," Abe said with a chortle. "I'm a happy man with a place of my own and plenty of good company. Couldn't ask for more."

Taylor snorted in the background, drawing Abe's attention.

"We can't all be highfalutin like the doc here. I'm just glad he's taken such a shine to you, little girl. Your Mama and Papa would be pleased."

Before Taylor could deny any personal interest, Sara Beth did it for him.

"We are just acquaintances," she insisted. "However, he is going to teach me all about medicine so

I can work with him at the orphanage. Isn't that wonderful?"

Abe looked surprised, then started to roar with laughter, tightly clasping his sides as if he were about to shake them apart. When he recovered enough to speak he said, "You? A doc? That'll be the day. Imagine. A woman doctor? Might as well move right into my collection. I can put you up next to the sea monkey or the mermaid. Yes, sirree."

She looked to Taylor. "I think it's time we left."

"I couldn't agree more." He had noticed that their presence was attracting far too much attention, especially since Abe had begun hooting and hollering, and he wanted to take her away before things got further out of hand.

"Luke," the doctor shouted. "Come on. We're leaving."

The boy came slowly, scuffing his feet on the dusty floorboards. "Aw. Do we hafta?"

"Yes," Sara Beth said firmly. "We have to."

In Taylor's opinion the boy was far from being as reformed as his sister seemed to believe. There might be hesitant compliance in his actions but he retained a defiant look, a posture that indicated he was inches from outright refusal.

Now was not the time to bring that up, of course, but Luke would bear watching. His young mind had obviously not yet grasped the gravity of the situation and he was still a danger to everyone. Any boy who would take money for betraying his sister was not going to change his ways after only one good talking-to. Nor was he likely to think things through himself and decide to do right in the future.

No, Taylor decided easily. That boy was trouble. All he had to do was figure out how to warn Sara Beth without alienating her completely. He would have felt a lot better about the situation if he'd had a clue how he should proceed.

Well, one problem at a time, he told himself as he escorted her and the boy back to his buggy. The sun was already so low over the bay that twilight was upon them. The sooner his charges got back to the orphanage the better.

Once he saw Sara Beth and Luke safely inside, he'd finish his rounds of patients in town and quit for the day. His practice had suffered greatly since he'd become so involved with the Reese family. Nevertheless, he was going to persevere until things were settled properly, although their modest estate might not be worth much by the time Bein got through milking it and they overcame the additional problem of government involvement.

None of that mattered in the grand scheme of things. There were some events over which man had little or no control, just like the flurries of earthquakes that kept shaking up the city. Taylor knew that. He also knew at this point there was nothing he could do to stop caring too much about what happened to Sara Beth and her siblings for his own good. It was as if he had been designated her protector without any option to decline.

Unfortunately, that task seemed to suit him so well he no longer had any desire to quit.

Ella McNeil was beside herself when Sara Beth and Luke finally arrived with the doctor. She pulled both her charges into her ample embrace as if they had been away for months. "Land sakes. I thought you'd never get back. What on earth is going on?"

"It's a long story. We're fine. Really, we are," Sara Beth assured her as Luke extricated himself and edged away. "Dr. Hayward has been escorting us."

"Fine kettle of fish." She glared at Taylor. "Don't you have a lick of sense? These poor things missed supper and evening devotions already."

Sara Beth noted that he had already politely removed his bowler and was trying to look suitably contrite. He was also failing miserably. She came to his defense.

"Actually, it was Luke who left first, on an errand for me, and if the doctor had not taken me down the hill to search for him, things might have turned out for the worse."

"Mercy me." Ella fanned herself with fluttery hands. "What happened?"

Choosing her words carefully, Sara Beth explained in detail while her brother sulked. When she was finished, she sighed. "Do you suppose Clara would mind if we looked for a bite to eat? I know I'm probably too late to help with the dishes and I don't want her to think ill of me."

"Of course she won't mind. You all just go out there and have whatever's left. Nobody will mind a bit."

"Come with us?" Sara Beth asked, addressing the doctor. "You haven't eaten either, have you?"

"No. I almost did. I had to leave the table before I was served."

Although he was smiling, she realized everything was her fault. "I'm so sorry. Let me fry you some eggs and side pork to make up for it."

"I'd love to stay, but duty calls," Taylor told her, making a slight bow before he put his hat back on his head. "I'll be by tomorrow and we'll look in on the children together."

"You haven't changed your mind about letting me help?" Her cheeks warmed. "I wondered, after the way Abe Warner acted."

Taylor smiled and Sara Beth felt extremely blessed by his beneficent expression.

"Abe has no idea how intelligent you are, Miss Reese. If he did, he wouldn't have laughed." He sobered. "I know it hurt your feelings. Just remember, there may come a day when your understanding of the practice of medicine will prove your mettle."

"I sincerely hope so." She offered her hand to him. "God's speed, Doctor. Be careful out there. The world is a far more unfriendly place than I had dreamed."

She stood in the half-open doorway as Taylor took his leave, climbed into his buggy and drove away. Her last statement kept echoing in her mind and heart. *Unfriendly?* More like perilous. And fearsome. And volatile beyond reason.

Sara Beth momentarily closed her eyes, offering up a silent prayer for the doctor's protection. He was so kind. So helpful. So…dear, her heart insisted.

Her eyes popped open and she stared into the dimness of the garden, not seeing any of what lay before her. Instead, her mind's eye was focused on the handsome doctor and all he had done for her, even agreeing to teach her the art of healing when so many other men would have laughed the same way Abe Warner had.

Dr. Hayward, *Taylor* in her heart, was more than her benefactor. He was special beyond words, beyond thoughts. It was probably a terrible sin to covet his presence and think so highly of him, but she couldn't help herself. The only thing she truly looked forward to was seeing him again. Listening to the timbre of his voice as it sent shivers up her spine. Perhaps even holding his hand the way she had that very evening.

She blinked, trying to clear her head. It was no use. She was besotted. Smitten. A hopeless romantic caught up in a tangle of intrigue and beginning to care less about her current trials than she did about one special gentleman.

"This will never do," Sara Beth insisted, taking a quick step backward and preparing to secure the heavy door for the night.

As it swung closed she heard a loud noise. It wasn't until she glanced up at the edge of the mahogany door and saw a splintered hole that she realized she had just been shot at!

"Well, did you get her?"

Scannell shook his head. "Naw. She ducked at the last minute and my man missed."

Bein cursed.

"Simmer down. We'll fix her. We fetched you her letter, didn't we?"

"A fat lot of good that does when she spent an hour talking to King at the *Bulletin*."

"He can be dealt with, too, you know."

The stylish businessman shook his head as he brushed invisible dust off the cuff of his jacket. "Not yet. We don't want to call too much attention to him or to his paper, especially not when the governor has sent Sherman to take over as major general of the second division of militia."

Chuckling, the sheriff snorted. "I wouldn't worry about Sherman. He'll be hamstrung by General Wool and maybe Farragut, too, if he asks the Navy for help. We're the Law and Order Party, remember?"

"Yes. And we have Governor Johnson hoodwinked. I just don't trust everyone to continue to act in my best interests. Neither should you."

"I don't see why you're so worried about one newspaperman. King doesn't control all the press."

"No, but he's influential with the right people. Remember, he was a banker until he lost his own fortune in the panic of '54. He made plenty of friends among the rich when he was one of them."

"So? He bleeds like every other man."

"I hope it won't come to that," Bein said. "Eliminating my partner was bad enough. Having poor Isabelle caught in the crossfire was inexcusable."

"Did you have a soft spot in your heart for her?" Scannell asked.

"None of your business. Just see that I'm kept abreast of any new developments and guard the Reese property until I tell you different."

"Yes, sir." He smiled slyly. "What about the girl? She's trouble and you know it. Do you want us to try for her again?"

"Not yet. Let's give it a few days and see what else happens. I'm curious about what King's actually planning to print and I don't want anyone to have reason to blame me for your sloppy work."

"Well, it's pretty confusin' and that's a fact. I can't hardly tell who's on our side and who's not."

"As long as you continue to take orders from me you'll be fine. Don't even think of selling out to the other side or you won't live long enough to spend whatever they pay you. Understand?"

"Yeah, yeah. You can trust me, Mr. Bein."

He lit a cheroot and blew smoke before he smiled and said, "I don't trust anybody but myself. Never have and never will. That was my late, lamented partner's problem. He trusted the wrong people." He chuckled. "And look what it got him."

Taylor arrived at the orphanage late the following afternoon and entered through the kitchen with the express goal of seeing Sara Beth. He wasn't disappointed.

Squealing with delight, she ran straight to him, stopping just inches from being in his arms once again.

He could tell from the expression on her face that she was embarrassed to have shown so much emotion. He could sympathize. When she'd raced across the room to greet him he had nearly acted on instinct and swept her into his embrace. *That* would have given Clara and Mattie plenty to gossip about, wouldn't it?

"How are you today, Miss Reese?" Taylor asked.

She gave a slight curtsey. "Fine, thank you, Doctor."

"I trust you slept well."

As he spoke he was peeking past Sara Beth at the older women, and it was clear to him that they were not fooled one bit. They both looked dreamy-eyed, as if they were watching a courtship rather than the conversation of two casual friends, as he'd intended.

"No. Not really," Sara Beth said, sobering and lightly touching his forearm. "Come with me. I want to show you something."

Puzzled, Taylor frowned. "Show me what? What's the matter?"

"You'll see." She led him to the heavy front door and slowly opened it, staying behind its bulk as she did so. "Don't stand in the open. Step back here, closer to me."

"I really don't think that's wise, do you?" he said, smiling and feeling decidedly ill at ease. The lovely young woman might not realize how her presence had begun to affect him, but that did not excuse him from behaving properly.

She grabbed his sleeve and pulled him aside. "I am not about to let your stubborn nature get you killed." Pointing, she added, "Look."

Aghast, he stared at the splintered wood. "Is that what I think it is?"

"If you guessed a bullet hole, then yes. It happened last night, after I bid you goodbye. Thankfully, the shot missed."

That was too much for Taylor. He drew her into his arms and held her close, oblivious to the lack of propriety. "Dear Lord. You might have been killed."

"Like my father and mother were," Sara Beth murmured. "I didn't see anyone out there. Maybe it was merely an accidental discharge of a firearm and I happened to be in the wrong place at the wrong time."

"Whatever the reason, you're not going outside again. Not until we figure out who is behind all this."

Instead of agreeing as he had hoped, she pushed him away and stepped back. "Don't be ridiculous. You can't be certain anyone was shooting at me. Besides, I attended church this morning with the others. We walked all the way and nothing bad happened."

That thought chilled Taylor to the bone. He grasped her shoulders to keep her facing him. "Do you believe you're safe merely because you're on your way to worship service? That's idiotic. So is assuming that the shot last night was an accident."

He took a deep breath, warring within himself to control his impulse to embrace her again. "If you didn't agree, you wouldn't have warned me to stand behind the door."

"Okay. So maybe I do think it was an attack. That still doesn't mean I have to live like a prisoner in a dungeon."

At the end of his patience and so worried he could hardly keep from trying to shake some sense into her, he dropped his arms to his sides, turned and walked away. "I'm going to make my rounds. Are you coming?"

He heard her soft footsteps and the rustle of her skirts behind him. What was he going to do with her? How was he going to convince her that she was in mortal danger? Surely she must not fully realize the gravity of the situation or she wouldn't be behaving so irrationally.

Not that he was any more sane, he told himself. Ever since he had first encountered Sara Beth Reese he had been acting as addled and erratic as a Sunday-dinner chicken with its neck wrung.

That colorful analogy did nothing to calm his fears. Neither did the way Sara Beth was acting. To look at her, a person would think she hadn't a care in the world.

He, on the other hand, was worried enough for both of them. If she continued to insist on going out, there was nothing he could do to protect her. Absolutely nothing.

Chapter Ten

The *Bulletin* had remained silent about the Reese situation for the past week. Each day, Sara Beth had eagerly scanned the evening edition and each time she had been disappointed.

Only Dr. Hayward's continuing encouragement and pleasing presence buoyed her spirits. He had taken to visiting the orphanage at least twice every day and she was delighted to see him, no matter what news he carried.

"I don't understand why your friend hasn't printed my story yet," she remarked as they tended to ailing children and administered a spoonful of Clara's homemade horehound cough elixir to each one.

"He'll get around to it," Taylor assured her.

"Right now he's in the middle of a series about corruption and is focusing on James Casey. I told you about Casey. He owns the *Herald*."

"Can't Mr. King cover more than one topic at a time?"

"The way he explained it, he figures it will be advantageous to clear the city of Casey's negative influence and then proceed with cleaning up the rest of the crooks who are in power, including Bein and his cohorts."

"Are his facts accurate?" She made a face that mimicked the expression of the child who had just tasted the cough cure. Truth to tell, the sinful atmosphere of the city was far more revolting to her than any bitter medicine. Just thinking about the dirty politics was enough to turn her stomach.

"Of course they are. James King is the most honest, careful editor in San Francisco. We're lucky to have him on our side."

She nodded, her expression grim. "Until I was wronged, I had never paid much attention to what went on at City Hall. I suppose many citizens are the same. We're too content to let sleeping dogs lie."

"These so-called dogs may well be rabid," Taylor countered. "Did you read any of the exposé on Casey?"

"Most of it. I can hardly believe that he was a

convicted criminal who served prison time in New York. He was elected city supervisor here by a landslide. That's incredible."

"I'd agree, if I didn't believe that the election was rigged like so many others have been." Washing his hands, Taylor dried them on a small towel before packing up his medical bag. "I told King he'd better be careful. A hardened criminal like Casey can be dangerous, especially if he's convinced he has nothing more to lose."

"What can he do? Surely the newspaper articles are not considered defamatory as long as they're true."

Taylor set his jaw. "He's threatened retribution in front of witnesses, for one thing. I wish I could get King to take the threats seriously. He's carrying his pistol with him at all times and watching where he goes and with whom, but that may not be enough."

"I disagree," Sara Beth said. "Casey wouldn't dare harm him, especially not after issuing public threats. He'd be blamed immediately and probably hung."

"Would he?" The doctor arched his eyebrows. "Even if Scannell arrested him, I doubt they could find a fair judge and jury for a trial. Casey would have half the town in his vest pocket to start with."

Sara Beth did not want to believe there was so

much evil all around her, yet the more she learned, the less she believed that she and her family would ever obtain justice.

Praise the Lord for a man like James King who believed her. "Do you suppose it would help if you and I visited the *Bulletin* office again?"

The look Taylor sent her was anything but supportive. "Don't be silly."

"I'm not anything of the kind," Sara Beth argued. "I'd like to talk with Mr. King again, that's all."

"And say what?"

"I don't know. I just feel so helpless, acting as if I'm in hiding. I need to get out, do something, even if it's futile. Can you understand that?"

"I understand it but that doesn't mean I think it's a sensible idea."

"Sensible or not, I want to go. I will go. With or without you."

Taylor sighed and nodded slowly. "All right. We're finished here. Go tell Mrs. McNeil we're going downtown. I'll drive you so you don't have to walk. The less time you're out on the streets, the better."

Her spirits soared. "Oh, thank you! I've felt so cooped up and frustrated staying inside. And it's a lovely, sunny afternoon. Perfect weather for a drive." She didn't care that she was grinning foolishly. "I'll get my shawl and meet you at the buggy."

We're going for a ride. Together. Sara Beth's heart was practically singing and her feet felt as if they barely touched the floor as she hurried to the small chest that held her personal things. She had managed to obtain a second presentable dress and Clara had loaned her several aprons to keep her clothing clean while she worked. Other than that, she had only her coat, a shawl, mother's reticule and…

That thought focused and brought Sara Beth up short. She had not looked inside her mother's purse since that awful night when some kindly stranger had handed it to her at the wharf. Mama had been carrying a small, single-shot pistol. If it was still there, as she hoped, it would provide a little extra protection.

True, it had not helped Mama. Not enough anyway. But any weapon of self-defense was better than being totally vulnerable.

The reticule lay in the bottom of the small storage chest, just where she'd stashed it. Sara Beth's heart pounded as she eased the drawstrings, opened the velvet-lined bag, then gingerly lifted the pistol to study it. To her dismay, it was not loaded.

Because Mama shot the attacker. Of course. That one bullet had found its mark and had served its purpose well.

The trouble was, she had no idea how to reload safely or where she would find ammunition if she did know how to fit a ball and powder properly into the tiny pistol. As it was, it was about as useful for defense as a hand-size rock would be.

Nevertheless, she slipped the gun into her pocket. Later, after she and the doctor had visited the newspaper office, she'd ask him about ammunition and enlist his expertise. Perhaps they could get it loaded tonight because without a suitable weapon, she *was as useless as that unloaded pistol*.

James King was not a foolish man. Nor was he fearful. He'd always been able to talk his way out of trouble, even in the face of apparently insurmountable odds.

Closing his editorial office, he checked his pocket watch as he descended the stairway on the west side of Montgomery Street. It was just past five. Mist from the bay was starting to roll in and the mournful sound of foghorns echoed off the tall, brick buildings of the business district as well as the surrounding hills.

The hair on the back of his neck suddenly prickled. He whirled. His eyes widened when he saw who was approaching. "What are you doing here?"

"I told you I'd kill you if I saw you," Casey said. He was pointing a revolver.

King held up his hands, palms out. It was too late to draw his own pistol. If he hoped to survive, he'd have to argue his way out of this. "Take it easy. I didn't print anything that wasn't true. It was only a matter of time until the whole story came out. You know that."

"All I know is that you've ruined everything," Casey said. He was eyeing the other man's bulging coat pocket. "Go ahead. Go for your pistol. I'm willing to shoot it out right here and now."

"Well, I'm not," King said, beginning to perspire beneath his top hat. "Be sensible, man."

At the last second, when he saw his adversary's eyes narrow and his flushed face tighten in a sneer, he knew he had underestimated Casey. The gun fired. King dropped, hit squarely in the left shoulder.

Before he lost consciousness he was briefly aware that his attacker was approaching. He could only hope and pray that the man did not intend to fire again and finish him where he lay.

Taylor and Sara Beth were almost to the intersection of Montgomery and Merchant streets when they heard a commotion.

She grasped the doctor's arm. "Was that a shot?"

"Sounded like it." He pulled the buggy to the side

of the road, passed her the reins and jumped out. "Stay here. I'll go check."

Before he disappeared around the corner of the nearby hotel, she had already made up her mind. She was not about to just sit there idle when he might need her help.

Unmindful of danger to her own person, she shed her shawl, carefully gathered her skirts and eased herself down by way of the small metal step at the side of the buggy. In his haste, Taylor had left without his medical bag. That provided a perfect excuse. She would deliver it to him.

What she encountered on Montgomery Street was utter chaos. Dozens of people were milling about. Women wept. Men cursed or shouted or laughed maniacally.

She stared. Her heart pounded and she was barely able to catch her breath. *Taylor. Where is Taylor?*

There! In the midst of the throng. That had to be him. Frantic, she pushed through the crowd and immediately saw the full effect of the carnage. The doctor was crouching next to the body of a well-dressed, middle-aged man. Off to the side, another man was being wrestled to a standstill by passersby. She didn't recognize the second person, but the victim was definitely James King from the *Bulletin*.

The whole scenario was an agonizing reminder of the way her parents had died. For an instant she relived their demise as if she were seeing it again. Would she never have peace? Would the terrible pain and sense of loss never fade?

Forcing herself to focus, Sara Beth blinked to clear her head. She must act. She would act. She willed her feet to carry her closer to the doctor and saw, to her great relief, that the victim, Mr. King, was still moving, although he was groaning and bleeding badly.

She thrust the medical bag at Taylor. "Here. You forgot this."

The swift look he gave her was chastening in spite of his obvious need of the instruments. "Thank you."

"You're welcome." This was the first time Sara Beth had been present when her mentor was doing anything other than taking temperatures or handing out doses of elixir. She was so fascinated by his deft movements that she momentarily forgot her own distress.

He pressed a thick pad against the patient's shoulder, then gestured to a couple of men loitering nearby. "We need to get him inside and into bed. Help me carry him to the closest hotel. You take his feet," he told the first. "And you and I will support his shoulders," he said, pointing to the second man. "I'll handle the injured side."

Following Taylor inside, toting his medical bag once again, Sara Beth wondered if she could have risen to the occasion as he had. Easing the discomfort of a child with a cold was one thing. Stopping a man from bleeding to death was quite another. Maybe Abe had been right to laugh at her lofty aspirations. Maybe she wasn't cut out to become a doctor.

Then again, although she had felt her stomach clench at the grisly sight and had momentarily relived the worst time of her life, she had not swooned the way some of the other women in the crowd had. On the contrary, she might be a bit shaky, but she was nonetheless alert and ready to do whatever Taylor told her to do—other than stay behind in the buggy.

She realized she was as stubborn as her brother—and as stubborn as her mother had been. The thought surprised her and she forced herself to focus on the situation at hand.

As the men struggled to carry their limp burden up the stairway and place him in a hotel room, Sara Beth hung back and studied the crowd. Some of those present seemed distressed over the editor's shooting. Many, however, were smiling and apparently enjoying the excitement. Worse, those who had captured the assailant had already released him and were behaving as if he had done nothing wrong! James Casey was hiding behind Sheriff Scannell as if the lawman was his personal shield.

Perhaps that was what Taylor had meant when he'd said they would have trouble finding a fair judge and jury. If such a panel were chosen from the men she observed here, there would be a very good chance that King's foe would be exonerated.

Her feet felt leaden and so did her heart as she finally proceeded up the stairs, pausing at the landing. This was wrong, so wrong. And yet it was happening right in front of her eyes. A good, honest man was injured and might be dying while his attacker had been released and was now standing with his cronies in the hotel lobby below, laughing, talking and smoking a cigar as if nothing untoward had occurred.

Her breath caught. In the rear of that throng, near the door, stood the smug-looking figure of William Bein. And he was leering at her.

Taylor was afraid for his friend. As soon as Sara Beth joined him with his medical bag, he held out a hand. "It's the subclavian artery. Give me the large hemostats. They're made like scissors only they clamp instead of cutting."

"I know what they look like."

She was not only quick to respond; she seemed quite calm amidst all the bedlam, further impressing Taylor with her bravery and fortitude.

As he worked to stem the bleeding and failed repeatedly to locate and clamp the damaged ends of the artery, he wondered how long poor James could last. It didn't look good. Not good at all. And there was little anyone could do.

Other doctors, older medical men, had been summoned. They shoved Taylor away and took his place. He would have fought for position if he had not already done all he could. Nuttall and Toland were good men, as surgeons went. Perhaps they would have more success by working as a team.

"Why are you backing off and letting those men tend to him?" Sara Beth asked, frowning as she handed Taylor a damp towel from the washstand so he could wipe his hands.

"Because there's nothing more I can do. I'd let old Abe Warner himself try if I thought it would help."

"I'm so sorry."

"Don't give up on him yet," Taylor insisted. Though he knew his friend probably didn't have much longer to live, he also knew that even while unconscious, James could likely hear and understand what was being said. Many a professor had impressed that fact upon him in medical school, citing instances where dying patients had rallied at the last instant and had later been irate at the conversations they had overheard during their supposed passing.

Leading her aside, Taylor spoke privately. "I need to get you back home but I can't leave James."

"Of course you can't. I wouldn't ask it of you. Besides, there may be some way we can assist those other doctors."

"Perhaps. Perhaps not." Even from where he and Sara Beth stood they could hear the others loudly discussing treatment. Nuttall was suggesting that they plug the wound with a sponge, much to Taylor's dismay.

"You can't do that," he insisted, stepping closer. "He'll die of infection. Haven't you read Semmelweis's papers?"

The others ignored him. Starting to turn away, he suddenly heard his friend moan and call his name.

"James?" Taylor pushed through and fell to his knees by the side of the bed. "I'm right here."

"Don't leave me," King pleaded, grasping Taylor's fingers so tightly the grip was painful. "In the name of all that's Holy, Hayward, don't leave me to these butchers."

"I've done all I can to stem the flow. We should let them try."

"I'm already a dead man. I know that," King said in a low, shaky voice. "Promise you'll see that Casey pays for murdering me."

Nodding, Taylor vowed that he would. In seconds, the other man was once again unconscious and had loosened his grip.

The young doctor rose and returned to Sara Beth. "When we came in, I think I spotted W. T. Coleman with some of the other men from the Vigilance Committee. If I can locate him, I'll have him take you home in my buggy."

"I should stay with you," she said, eyeing the pompous other doctors. "You might need moral support, and besides, William Bein was downstairs the last time I looked."

"All the more reason for you to take advantage of the distraction provided by the crowd. I may be here for a long time. There's no sense both of us holding vigil."

"All right. Whatever you think is best."

"Thank you for understanding," Taylor said, gently taking both her hands and holding them. "If I don't have your safety to worry about I'll be better able to think, to help look after James properly."

"I heard him say he thought he was dying," she whispered. "Isn't that a bad attitude to foster?"

"Not if it's true." Taylor released her and started

to turn toward the closed door that led into the hallway. "I'd much rather see a man prepare himself to meet his Maker than die suddenly and not have a chance to repent."

The moment those words were spoken he rued them. Sara Beth's mother and father might have faced exactly that fate and, judging by the pained expression on her face, she had reached the same conclusion.

"I'm sorry. I didn't mean—"

"I know. And I agree. No man can predict when his time is near. I know Mama's soul was right with God and I can't imagine divine providence separating two people who loved each other as dearly as she and Papa Robert did."

"All right. Stay up here with James and the others where you'll be safe. I'll locate W.T. or one of his trustworthy men and arrange an escort."

"I don't suppose you'd consider just letting me walk home?"

"Not in a million years," the doctor said flatly.

He was not a bit surprised when Sara Beth answered, "That's what I thought."

Chapter Eleven

As far as Sara Beth was concerned, she was not in need of cosseting. However, given the stress Taylor Hayward was currently under, she figured it would be best to go along with his ideas and allow Mr. Coleman to see her home.

The only off-putting element was the degree of nervousness and mental distraction the middle-aged businessman was displaying as he drove. To look at his pale skin, perspiring brow and glassy eyes, a person would think he was the one who had just been shot instead of James King.

He brought the doctor's buggy to a stop in front of the orphanage without comment, leaving Sara Beth wondering if he had even noticed where they were.

She offered her hand. When he seemed to ignore the friendly gesture, she simply gathered her skirts and climbed out of the buggy unassisted before saying, "Thank you for bringing me home, sir. Will you be returning to the hotel now?"

"What? Oh, I suppose so." His hand was trembling as he touched the brim of his hat politely. "Evening, miss."

Watching the familiar buggy drive away, Sara Beth realized that she was not lamenting its departure the way she usually did, which was, of course, because Mr. Coleman was driving instead of Taylor Hayward.

Her heart ached for the young doctor. How difficult it must be to tend to a close friend and be unable to help him. Since the very thought of being in that untenable position caused her anguish, how must Taylor feel to be facing it in reality?

How long would poor James King linger? she wondered as she entered the orphanage. He had endured so much suffering already that she was almost prepared to pray the Lord took him home soon, before he had to bear more. In that respect, she supposed her parents had been blessed, if one could imagine death being a positive event. How unbelievers coped with such a loss was unimaginable. No wonder so many folks, like Abe Warner, for instance, professed faith even if they chose not to attend church.

Entering the kitchen, she smiled at Clara. "I'm back. Is there anything I can do to help you and Mattie?"

"There's always somethin'," the heavyset woman answered soberly. "But I think you should check with Ella first."

Clara's lack of joviality took Sara Beth aback. "Why? What's wrong?"

"You'd best talk to Ella. I don't want to be carrying tales, if you know what I mean."

"No, I don't know what you mean," Sara Beth said. "Tell me. Please?"

Sighing, the cook dried her hands on her apron and nodded. "All right. It's that brother of yours. Luke. He snuck off right after you left and hasn't come back."

"Oh, dear!"

She wheeled and ran for the front of the mansion. Luke was gone. And chances were good that if he'd made it all the way into the city, he'd heard the rumors and had done what so many others had. He'd followed the crowds to the scene of the shooting to see for himself what all the excitement was about.

Locating Mrs. McNeil in the parlor, Sara Beth

immediately grasped her hand. "What happened to Luke? When did he leave? How long has he been gone?"

Just then, a mild tremor shook the house, making the chandelier sway. Sara Beth was so used to the shaking and rumbling of the earth beneath the city that she barely took notice.

Ella McNeil, however, gave a little shriek and froze, listening and waiting for more. "Mercy. I hate it when that happens."

"It's over," Sara Beth insisted. "What about Luke?"

"Yes, Luke." The matron made a sour face. "I don't know what we're going to do about that boy. I tried to reason with him, but I might as well have been talking to the garden wall."

"What did he say? Clara told me he left right after I went with the doctor."

"That's right. He insisted that if you could leave, he could, too. He said he wanted to go home. I tried to explain that your old house was all shut up and guarded but he refused to listen to me."

"Is that where he was headed? Are you sure?"

"I reckon so." She held tight to Sara Beth's hand when the younger woman tried to pull away. "I've sent one of the men from the Vigilance Committee to look for him. Luke will be fine. I don't want you running off to find him, you hear?"

"Who did you send? Does the man even know what Luke looks like? Does he?" She knew her voice was rising and her tone panicked but she couldn't help it. "I have to go. Don't you see? Luke will listen to me."

In her deepest heart she hoped that conclusion was correct. She realized that she had erred when she'd failed to inform the two oldest boys of William Bein's treachery. As far as Luke and Mathias knew, *Uncle Will* was still to be trusted. Given that fact, there was every chance that if they chanced to meet, Luke would go willingly with that appalling man.

And then what? she asked herself, her eyes growing misty. Someone had already tried to kidnap Luke once. If anything like that happened again and she wasn't around to rescue him, what would become of her poor brother?

She knew she should be furious at Luke for disobeying and leaving the orphanage grounds, yet she could sympathize with his urge to return to their once happy home. If that was all he did, and if he was not spotted by the guards the sheriff had placed at the property, then perhaps he would return unscathed.

Tears brimmed and slipped down her cheeks. She had promised Taylor that she would stay on the grounds of the Ladies' Protection and Relief Society for refuge. Like it or not, she was going to have to break that vow. She must track down her brother and see him safely back to the orphanage. There was no other sensible option.

She paused. Her eyes widened. In all the confusion and drama surrounding the assassination attempt, she had neglected to find out how to load her mother's pistol or obtain the means to do so. Once again, she would be making the journey down the hill unarmed.

King had lapsed into unconsciousness and stayed there, even after Dr. Nuttall's sponge had stanched the bleeding. If Taylor had been in charge he would not have risked the onset of sepsis by using that method, but he had to admit that, for the moment, his friend was still breathing.

With the unconscious man fading, and the other doctors clearly in charge, Taylor decided to leave long enough to check with Coleman and make sure Sara Beth had arrived safely at the orphanage.

Coleman was not in his office. Taylor found the head of the Vigilance Committee leading a rally at the Turn Verein Hall on Bush Street.

Taylor had just reached the hall when another party arrived, led by Governor Johnson and a wiry military man he soon realized was Major General Sherman. While their entourage was made to wait, Taylor was ushered inside to see Coleman.

The meeting room was filled with men who were risking their lives and their businesses by gathering this way, even though the roster of the committee was kept by number rather than given name.

"Did you get her home?" Taylor asked.

"What?"

"The girl. Miss Reese. Is she safe?"

Coleman took out a monogrammed handkerchief and mopped his brow. "Safer than any of us are. Did you see who's waiting to interview me?"

"Yes. So? You're not doing anything wrong. None of us are. There's no law against holding a meeting."

"There is if you're planning vigilante justice," Coleman said in a low voice. "How's King?"

"Near death. It won't be long."

"That's what I was afraid of."

Taylor eyed the throng. Many were watching their conversation with grim expressions. It looked to him as if Coleman was about to lose control of the mob.

"Aren't you going to go see what the governor wants?" the doctor asked.

"I suppose I have no choice. What if he orders

us to disband? I'll never be able to convince these men that they shouldn't act, especially if King dies."

"One thing at a time," Taylor said, clapping him on the back. "Come on. I'll go with you to beard the lions. I can tell them about King's condition and his declaration that Casey shot him."

"Think it will matter?"

"I certainly hope so. I'd hate to be stuck between justice and the law."

"Scannell, you mean?"

"Him and Judge Norton. I don't trust either of them, even though the judge does have a good reputation."

"At least the grand jury is in session. We may be able to convince them to indict Casey quickly and avoid a riot."

"It'll have to be fast," Coleman replied. "These men are at the end of their ropes and I can't say I blame them."

The afternoon wind off the Pacific was chilling, making Sara Beth wish she had remembered to grab her shawl from the buggy. She hugged herself, wrapping her arms tight to ward off the shivers. It was not only the temperature and the breeze that were making her cold; it was also thoughts of her brother. Luke was not a bad person; he was simply naive. All the Reese children, herself included, had been sheltered from reality and were therefore unprepared to discern evil and properly deal with it.

How was she going to help Luke if he got into trouble again? She didn't have a plan, but she would take advantage of the fact that she was young and female and would attract far less attention than a grown man, particularly if she kept her eyes downcast and didn't get in anyone's way. Such subservient behavior was contrary to her nature. That didn't matter. Not now. Not when Luke was out there somewhere, alone and probably courting danger once again.

She hurried along the boarded walkway that led to her former home on Pike Street, darting behind a tree as soon as she had the place in sight. From that vantage point she could see most of the property, at least the front and one side. It looked deserted. Then again, the guards might be inside, sitting in Papa's chair, propping their dirty boots on Mama's needlepoint-covered footstool and spitting tobacco juice on the floor.

"That's so wrong," she murmured as those vivid imaginings whirled in her mind. "No one has a right to desecrate our family home. If my brothers and I don't get it back, no one should have it." She gritted her teeth. "Especially not William Bein."

Long minutes passed. There was no sign of life at the house or the laboratory that made up one wing. Not only were there apparently no guards, there was also no sign of Luke, which could be good news or bad, depending on whether he had come here at all.

Stepping out from behind the tree, Sara Beth started to inch closer. A flash of movement in the bushes caught her eye. She froze, staring and praying that she had not alerted a hidden adversary.

The crouching figure moved. It was small. Too small to be one of the sheriff's men.

It was Luke! He was trying to pry open a window near Papa's assay office.

Rather than call out and startle him or call attention to either of them, she hiked her skirts above her toes and raced across the intervening distance. The boy was just lifting the sash when she clamped a hand on his shoulder.

He screamed like a frightened girl.

"Hush," she ordered in a hoarse whisper as she pressed her free hand over his mouth. "It's me. Sara Beth."

Instead of listening, Luke tried to bite her palm.

"Stop that!"

The boy was panting and wide-eyed in panic when she let him go. To her shock and disappointment, he started to curse a blue streak.

"Where did you learn such terrible language?"

"What do you care?"

"I care enough to have followed you here," she said flatly. "Now come with me. We're going home."

"I am home," Luke said, pouting. "I want my things. I'm going to go get them. You can't stop me."

She grabbed him and pulled him down into the bushes beside her just as a shadow crossed in front of the window. "Quiet. I didn't spot any guards on the porch but I just saw something inside. Unless you want to be kidnapped again and hauled off to goodness knows where, I suggest you button your lip."

"I don't see nobody."

"Anybody," she corrected. "I don't now either. Let's go check some of the other windows."

To her relief, the boy seemed agreeable. "Okay. You go that way and I'll—"

"Oh, no, you don't," Sara Beth said. "We're staying together. If you're right and there's no one inside, then I'll help you get your personal belongings. I'd like some of mine, too. And clothing for the others. But if we see guards we're leaving. Is that clear?"

"I guess."

"Good. And while I'm thinking about this whole situation, I need to tell you a few things about *Uncle Will*." As she watched her brother's expression she found his apparent lack of concern surprising. Luke had always acted as if he worshipped that man, so why was he now apparently feigning disinterest?

"William Bein is the reason why we can't live here," Sara Beth said. "He told me he owns the house and everything in it. He's the one who's responsible for the sheriff keeping a guard on it."

"I don't believe you."

"I had trouble accepting it, too," she said, nodding and looking directly into his wide-eyed gaze. "But it's true. All of it. Mama and Papa trusted him and he betrayed them." She hesitated, weighing her words before she added, "I even suspect that he may somehow be responsible for their murders."

"No!"

"Yes. He even tried to ship us back east. I saw the boat tickets with my own eyes."

Weeping, the boy tore himself from her grasp and ran. The only reason she didn't immediately race after him was that he had headed back the way they'd come, in the direction of the orphanage.

All she had to do was follow and hope that no

one with nefarious connections spotted her or Luke on the street, alone and unprotected.

She sighed. Gone was her joy in living, her sense of belonging in the city by the bay. Her childhood had been one of gladness, even before Papa Robert had married Mama, thanks to the benevolence of the Ladies' Protection Society. As an adult, however, she saw what her mother had seen. The orphanage was not a place where she would choose to stay if she had any other options. It was shelter, yes, but it would never be a real home.

Shivering, she once again folded her arms and began to trudge up the hill. In the distance, the mournful sounds of foghorns blended into a gloomy symphony that suited her mood perfectly.

Shadows were deepening, heralding a dismal end of the formerly lovely day. At the base of the hill, she heard a fuss. Men were shouting. Many were cursing at the top of their lungs, much to her dismay. What in the world could be wrong?

She heard someone shouting about the *Bulletin* and surmised that the ruckus stemmed from the shooting of its editor. Pausing to look back, she watched the crowd grow, saw torches, heard guns firing and hoped they were being shot into the air rather than into other men.

Frissons of terror gripped her as more and more

people ran past her and joined the mob. She was jostled. Shoved out of the way and off the walk into the muddy street.

Struggling to keep her balance and also dodge the passing throng, she felt herself falter. Someone gallantly righted her. She turned to offer thanks. Her jaw dropped.

Sheriff Scannell had hold of her arm and was grinning like a naughty little boy with a frog caught on his gigging fork.

"Let me go," Sara Beth demanded.

The sheriff laughed. "You're going all right. You're going with me to jail."

"Why? I haven't done anything wrong."

"Breaking into a house that belongs to the government and trying to steal gold ain't nothing, little lady. Don't try to deny it. I seen you with my own eyes."

Chapter Twelve

"Where is she? Where has she gone?" Taylor shouted. "How could you let her leave like that?"

Ella was near tears and wringing her hands. "I didn't *let* her. She went after the boy. What could I do?"

"Which way was she headed?"

"Toward their old house, I reckon. At least that's what she said."

"All right. If I don't find her and she comes back by herself, keep her here. There's trouble brewing and I don't want her caught in it."

"What kind of trouble?"

He figured it was better to frighten the matron with the truth than to let her blunder into danger due to ignorance. "Mob justice," he said. "The Vigilance Committee is planning to issue an official proclamation and try to take this city back from the powers of corruption. In the meantime, I suspect there will be violence."

"Mercy. Miss Sara Beth might be caught in the middle."

"My conclusion exactly," the doctor said.

He dashed out the door and vaulted into his buggy. The horse seemed to sense his anxiety. It pranced and pawed at the ground. Taylor eschewed the use of a whip in most cases, but this time he cracked it in the air above the horse's back and shouted, "Get up!"

The buggy careened out of the drive and into the street. Wagon traffic was unusually light, due, he surmised, to the turmoil closer to the city center. The number of citizens filling the wide streets multiplied as he traveled west until he could barely steer a safe path through the pedestrians.

It was all he could do to keep himself from plunging his rig into the crowd and trying to part it the way Moses had parted the Red Sea. Such a radical move was against the oath he had taken as a healer. He couldn't bring himself to chance harming anyone, yet he saw no way to get closer and hopefully locate Sara Beth if he didn't forge ahead.

Standing in the buggy, he scanned the thronging masses. His nervous horse wanted to run but he held him in check. Most of the people in the street were men. That should make finding her easier. That, and the fact that she had no hat or bonnet and therefore her reddish hair would stand out.

He was about to give up and climb down when he saw her. "Sara Beth! Over here," he shouted.

She turned her head, but instead of stopping and coming to him she continued to press on in the opposite direction.

In seconds, Taylor understood why. She was being held prisoner! Sheriff Scannell was dragging her away by the arm.

The buggy whip was in Taylor's hand. His grip tightened. Urging the horse forward, he cracked the whip repeatedly to clear a path. "Out of my way. Move," he yelled.

The tactic was successful enough to bring him within whipping distance of the sheriff. Giving no thought to his own culpability, he reached out and stung Scannell on his ear.

With a shout, the burly sheriff clapped a hand over that side of his face and raised his other arm to fend off more lashing. That was enough to give Sara Beth a chance to escape. She ran straight for the doctor's buggy.

Taylor gave her a hand up and pushed her into the seat, then flicked the whip one more time to

keep Scannell occupied before he snapped the reins
and gave the fractious horse its head.

"Hang on!"

"How did you find me?"

"Divine providence," Taylor shouted. "Keep
your head down."

His wasn't the only rig racing through the city
streets. Bedlam reigned. Women screamed. Men
scuffled and cursed. Mayor Van Ness had promised
that troops under Sherman would contain this
trouble, but it was clear that the army didn't have
nearly enough men on hand to keep the peace, no
matter what orders the general gave.

As far as Taylor was concerned, that meant only
one thing. The revolt had begun. And the only safe
place nearby would be Vigilance Committee headquarters on Clay Street. There, a makeshift fortification was being constructed out of sandbags in
preparation for standing off the troops, if necessary,
not to mention the so-called Law and Order party
that the sheriff represented.

"Where are we going?" Sara Beth screamed.

"The closest safe place."

"What about Luke?"

Taylor did his best to contain his fury, but he
could tell she was sensing it in spite of his best
efforts because she didn't argue when he looked her

in the eye and said sternly, "Believe me, Luke is the least of our worries right now."

Sara Beth had never seen the city in such an uproar, not even during one of the mild earthquakes that so often shook its citizens. This was different. This sense of disaster would not abate as soon as some worrisome tremors stopped.

She hung tightly to the edge of the buggy seat and braced herself. Their trip consisted of periods of breakneck speed interspersed with zigzagging around other wagons, an occasional omnibus and men on horseback as well as people on foot. It looked as if every one of San Francisco's eight thousand citizens was on the street at the same time. Some of the Chinese had even strayed from their usual section of the city and were mingling without censure, much to her surprise.

It was as if the entire city had gone mad and she was trapped amidst the mass hysteria. Praise God that the doctor had come after her, or there was no telling what the sheriff might have done, especially since there seemed to be no real law left.

She tensed as Taylor turned onto Clay Street and reined in at an opening in a row of sandbags piled as high as a man's shoulders.

"You get off here," he said.

"Why? Where are you going?"

"To check on King and then go look for your brother."

She reached for his arm and held tight. "Please don't leave me. Not now. Not when this is happening."

"You'll be safe in there with the Vigilance Committee," Taylor told her, pointing.

Her heart gave a sharp jolt and her already speeding pulse increased as he suddenly opened his arms and drew her into his embrace. She laid her head on his shoulder. "This is all my fault. I never should have gone after Luke. I just didn't know what else to do."

"You're responsible for him. I understand why you went looking. I just wish you'd gotten off the streets before this situation exploded."

"What's going on, anyway? Why are the people so upset?"

"This has been brewing for a long time," he said. "It was the shooting of King that brought it to a head."

"Is he dead?" Sara Beth hoped it was not so because that would mean that Taylor had lost a good friend.

"Probably," he answered softly. "Either way, if Casey doesn't have to stand trial, there will be more bloodshed." He gave her a brief squeeze. "I'll be back for you as soon as I can. There may be a curfew tonight. If there is, we'll have to figure out another way to get you back to the orphanage."

He climbed down and reached for her. Sara Beth placed her hands on his shoulders and let him lift her by the waist, setting her on the walkway in front of the vigilante headquarters.

"Take care of her," he told one of the nearby men. "W.T. knows who she is and why she needs to be here."

Her eyes filled with tears and she choked back a sob as she watched her rescuer climb back into his buggy and drive off. She cared for him. Deeply. And she had never even spoken his first name aloud, let alone confessed her burgeoning affection. When Taylor returned she would do so, she vowed as the strange man took her arm and escorted her inside the building.

In her heart she couldn't help adding, *If he returned.*

Taylor located Luke hanging around the docks in the company of some older, tough-looking youths, made certain the boy was once again confined at the orphanage, then headed back to claim Sara Beth.

She greeted him with so much overt emotion he hardly knew how to respond. As she clung to him and wept, he gently enfolded her in his embrace. Was she truly so enamored of him, he wondered, or was she simply reacting to the fright she had experienced?

He didn't know, nor was he sure he should press her about it. They had only been acquainted for a few weeks and although they had worked well together, he still couldn't accept anything more. He had his work. And she had her family's welfare to consider. The little he earned from his practice wouldn't come close to supporting her and her brothers in a proper manner.

Finally, she dried her eyes on the handkerchief he offered and apologized. "I'm sorry. I was just worried sick about you."

"I'm fine. And so is your brother. I gave him another good scolding and left him under Mrs. McNeil's watchful eye. She's locked him in the boys' ward. He won't get away again."

"Oh, dear." Sniffling, she shook her head. "I'm afraid Luke will see that as a challenge and double his efforts to escape. I don't know what to do with him."

"One crisis at a time," Taylor said, taking her hand and smiling. "The mob in the street has dispersed since they heard that King is still breathing and Casey has been hauled off to jail, mostly for his own safety, I assume. Things have quieted down enough that I can drive you home."

"All right. If you say so."

"I should be angry with you, you know."

I know," Sara Beth said, averting her gaze. "But you're not, are you? Not really."

There was no way Taylor could overlook the sweetness of her smile or the blush on her fair cheeks. Her hair had become mussed during her ordeal and the loose curls made her look like an endearing moppet. "No," he said. "I'm not."

Her grin spread and her green eyes twinkled mischievously. "Good. I'd be terribly sad if you were."

"Sad enough to behave and stay safely away from the city center for a while?"

"Well…"

Her soft drawl and the way she was gazing into his eyes made him melt inside like butter on a summer's day. This amazing young woman had led a sheltered life until mere weeks ago, yet she had coped and had blossomed in spite of the trials she'd been forced to endure. Many a man would have folded under less pressure.

His gut twisted as she laughed lightly. "Don't look so worried. I promise I shall behave as well as is sensible."

"That's what worries me," he quipped. When she reached up and gently caressed his cheek his knees nearly buckled.

"Sweet, sweet man," Sara Beth said. "You are so very dear to me."

"You're just overwrought," Taylor told her. "After things settle down and we get your inheritance back, you won't feel that way."

The crestfallen look that came over her cut him to the quick and affirmed his suspicion that she was growing far too fond of him. That would never do. Once she was again part of the landed gentry of the city, she would have her choice of many suitors who could add to her holdings and support her properly.

"Is there no swain waiting for you?" he asked.

"Papa was asked for my hand in marriage recently," she said, squaring her shoulders and lifting her chin to look at him with pride. "I refused the proposal."

"Why? Was the man unsuitable?"

"I suppose not," she replied. "I simply didn't love him."

"Perhaps you should reconsider."

He could tell by the misty look in her eyes that she not only did not think his idea had merit, she was hurt by the suggestion. That meant only one thing. Sara Beth Reese had set her cap for him.

Unfortunately, that distressing conclusion also warmed his heart and made him feel even more attracted to her than he had before.

The ensuing few days seemed to creep by for Sara Beth. Tom King, James's brother, had taken over the publication of the *Bulletin* and its editorials stirred up more unrest than they had before the shooting, especially once James King passed away.

The poor man had lingered at death's door longer than anyone had imagined he would, and in the interim a tenuous peace had returned to the city. In the end, his demise was caused, as Taylor had feared, by a raging infection.

According to the current stories in the newspapers, Casey's defense attorney was claiming that the death was brought about by the improper actions of King's doctors, not by the initial shooting.

That made Sara Beth furious. She could see no way that any judge or jury would believe such nonsense. If the bullet had not been fired in the first place, there would have been no wound to get infected.

She said as much when Taylor Hayward finally returned to the orphanage. He had been conspicuously absent since she had confessed her tender feelings toward him, leading her to conclude that he did not share them as she had hoped. Nevertheless, she still wanted to assist him, so she proceeded to do so, behaving as if her heart had not been broken.

"What's the word on the Casey trial?" she asked, following him down the hall and hoping that making small talk would relieve some of the tension she felt between them.

"Nothing new. Dr. Toland took the stand and swore under oath that it was that sponge in the wound that killed King, not the shooting."

"That's a ridiculous conclusion."

"I agree," Taylor said. "Hopefully the judge will, too."

"What about my house? Now that the *Bulletin* is only concerned with the King murder, what are my chances of getting justice?"

"I don't know. Word on the street is that Bein is being investigated for a theft originally blamed only on your father. If they can pin any part of the crime on him, you should have a better chance to eventually lay claim to your property."

"What about Papa Robert's good name? I can't just stand by and let him be vilified."

"I don't see how you'd ever prove his innocence. Not unless Bein confessed and exonerated him."

"Then that's what I shall pray for," she said flatly,

keeping the rest of her thoughts to herself. There had to be some way she could help, something she could do. But what? And how could she be of any use as long as she was cooped up like a prisoner in this stone fortress of a mansion?

If Taylor hadn't been so deeply involved in the Vigilance Committee, she might have petitioned them to champion her cause. As things stood, however, she was certain he would intercept her plea and tell the others that it was a hopeless situation.

Sighing, she realized that was probably a correct conclusion. It was a useless fight. She was barely old enough to be listened to, even if she had been a man, and since she was only a woman she had zero chance of being taken seriously.

One more letter, she decided. She would pen one more letter, this time to Tom King, and hope he listened half as well as his elder brother had. If she could tie her problems to those of the rest of the city, perhaps he would print what she had to say.

And this time she would not ask Taylor Hayward to deliver the letter. Nor would she trust Luke.

This time, she would take it to the editor herself, even if she had to wear a disguise and sneak in his back door to do so.

Chapter Thirteen

The temporary fortification surrounding the building on Clay Street was made up of stacks of sandbags, planks, overturned wagons and anything else the vigilantes could lay their hands on. They had even managed to appropriate a cannon and place it conspicuously at the corner near Front Street, a further demonstration of their power.

Before the buttressing was half completed it had already been nicknamed "Fort Gunnybags," much to the amusement of its builders.

Some of the men involved had served in the California militia and had assisted Fremont during the Mexican War. It was they who had formed the vigilantes into platoons and marched them through the streets like regular troops.

Taylor Hayward didn't choose to train with them, but he did begin to stockpile bandages and medicine in preparation for the battle he was certain would ensue, especially since W.T.'s command had been usurped by a younger, less level-headed man named Seymour.

It was he who brought the bad news. "It's over, boys. Time to march," Seymour shouted as he burst into the hall.

Listening, Taylor felt his blood run cold.

"Casey got off scot-free," the excited courier explained, cursing. "They ruled with Toland that it was the use of the sponge that killed James King."

As Taylor listened to the grumbling all around him it became clear that this was not going to be an occasion for negotiation. These men were irate. As long as they had each other for moral support there would be no reasoning with them. Nevertheless, he tried.

"It's the law, boys. We may not like it but it's legal."

"Only if we stand here jabbering and don't act," Seymour shouted. He raised his fist and gave a rallying cry. "Justice for our brother!"

"Justice. Justice," echoed from the walls and rattled the windows. Taylor knew better than to intercede further. Not only had he lost a great friend, San Francisco had lost a champion for true equality. He wasn't going to take part in a lynching but he wasn't fool enough to stand in the way of such a volatile throng, either.

Stepping aside, he watched the members of the Vigilance Committee crowd out the door, spill into the streets and form ranks. They could very well be marching to their deaths, yet they stepped boldly. James King had tried to clean up the city with his words. These men were determined to do so with their guns. Who was to say that either way was totally wrong? Being a pacifist had certainly not done the editor any good. Yet Taylor couldn't agree that taking the law into their own hands was right, either.

"Casey is guilty," he reminded himself, hoping that the vigilantes would at least hold another trial. A fair one. If Coleman had still been in charge that was exactly what would have happened. Unfortunately, that man's reluctance to wage war had been his undoing and he was now relegated to the background and being summarily ignored.

As Taylor climbed to the rooftop to gain a better vantage point, he was thankful that he had gotten Sara Beth out of the committee headquarters long before all this had come to a head. It was highly unlikely that the violence would spread beyond these few blocks near the city center and endanger the orphanage. Once the posse felt that justice had been served, the furor would die down. At least he hoped it would. If the riots continued long enough, Sherman might have time to join with General Wool in Benecia and actually muster enough armed men to physically put down the uprising. Then more men would die needlessly.

The ranks of armed volunteers were marching up Broadway in orderly fashion, heading toward the jail. Crowds of onlookers had already gathered in the lower streets and all the way up Telegraph Hill, as if they'd known what would occur once Casey was acquitted.

To the doctor's amazement, the scene was far less chaotic than it had been before. It was a stunning sight. The citizens may as well have been lining up to view a parade. Some waved handkerchiefs while others held bear flags of California or the Stars and Stripes.

He looked down, peering over the edge of the roof. Someone had already thrown a knotted rope across a beam that jutted from the front of the building.

It was tied in the shape of a noose.

Although Sara Beth was awed by the size of the crowd, she felt no fear. Not only was she wearing Ella's copious cloak and hood to hide her identity, these people were behaving in a far more orderly fashion than the previous mob had.

They were all moving along briskly, yet not pushing or acting angry. On the contrary, many looked relieved and expectant. She had heard that King's funeral had taken place the previous Sunday, so she couldn't imagine what would have brought all these folks into the streets at once.

Curious, she spoke to a nearby woman. "What's going on? What's happened?"

"There's gonna finally be a hangin'," the woman said, smiling. "Imagine that."

"A hanging? Today? Did they judge Casey guilty?"

"Naw. Leastwise not in court. But our brave boys will take care of that shameful mistake."

A knot of fear formed in Sara Beth's stomach. That news could mean only one thing. The law had failed and the Vigilance Committee had gone into action.

Hesitating, she stepped aside to think. If she proceeded to the newspaper office at a time like this there would probably be no one there to talk to, let alone receive her letter. All the reporters and everyone else would be in the streets, watching and waiting to see what happened.

To her dismay and disappointment she, too,

wanted to watch. Perhaps it was a flaw in her character or a lack within her Christian walk, she mused. Then again, maybe she was just like everyone else. She wanted to see justice done for a change.

Looking right and left, Sara Beth realized that no one was paying the least attention to her since she'd donned that dark, worn cape and hood. Wearing it made her feel a hundred years old but she didn't care as long as it kept her safe while she was out and about.

Did she dare proceed with the others? She sighed, undecided. The sensible thing to do would be to return to the orphanage and wait for Taylor to bring news of the hanging. Would he? She had her doubts. He had been acting so distant lately she wasn't sure he'd bother to inform her, even if he were free to do so.

And he might need her help, she reasoned, her mind made up. If there were wounded, which there were likely to be, she could assist him as his nurse.

"He's definitely going to need me," Sara Beth said firmly as she stepped out and rejoined the throng. "I belong at his side."

To her chagrin she immediately remembered the promise she had made to him. She was supposed to stay out of the city. She was bound to the orphanage by her vows. If she didn't go back and do as he'd told her to, he might be very angry.

She shook her head, her lips pressed into a thin line. "No. I have to go on. Taylor needs me."

And I need to be with him, she added silently, ruefully. She craved the doctor's presence the way a drowning person longs for a gulp of air.

That realization shook her to the core. In the space of a few weeks he had become so much a part of her that it was impossible to banish him from her thoughts. She knew, no matter what happened, she would never be the same person she'd been before meeting him.

And in her heart of hearts she also knew that their chances of finding happiness together were slim. When the current crises were past, there would be no need for him to watch over her. And perhaps there would also be no need for her to remain at the orphanage, where she encountered him so often.

That was the saddest thing of all. Attaining her goals for herself and her brothers would mean letting go of her dreams of working with the doctor and eventually becoming a nurse—or even a full-fledged doctor. She could not hope to support a household without income. Thinking of practicing medicine had been a lovely reverie, but it was no more than that. She knew where she ultimately belonged.

Right now, however, she was needed at the Vigilance Committee headquarters. And it was there she would go. As the Good Book said, "The cares of the day are sufficient." She would worry about her future at a later date.

The crowd in the street parted to make way for a commandeered freight wagon containing the prisoners. James Casey had been liberated from the sheriff and was accompanied by a man named Charles Cora, another murderer who was awaiting retrial for killing a U.S. marshal.

Taylor had been praying silently that no innocent people would be injured and, as far as he could tell, his pleas had been answered.

The wagon stopped just outside the sandbagged fortifications and the guards admitted their fellows as well as the two prisoners.

He could hear shouting and could tell that there was a kangaroo court convening below. It didn't take long for a unanimous verdict.

"Guilty. Hang 'em," the crowd shouted.

"Where's the doc?" someone yelled. "We need him to tell us when they're good and dead."

Others disagreed loudly, much to Taylor's relief.

It was his job to save life, not take it, and he didn't want any part of the hangings. Yes, he knew the men were guilty. And yes, he wanted justice. Desperately. He simply wasn't willing to dish it out without official sanction.

Turning, he started down the stairs. Others met him on the landing.

"C'mon, Doc. We're gettin' ready."

"I know. Are you sure about this?"

The vigilante sneered at him. "King was your friend. Don't you care that his murderer was gonna go free?"

"Of course I care. I'd just like to see this done lawfully, that's all. What about turning the prisoners over to the army?"

One of the men laughed and cursed, then elbowed his companion. "Let's go. He's got no stomach for justice."

They're right in this instance, Taylor thought as he stood there and watched them hurry back outside. *I can't believe God wants me to take a life when I've spent so many years trying to save them.*

And speaking of saving lives, I have the orphan children to think of. They need me, too. If I'm arrested for being a part of all this, who will look after them?

Huffing, he called himself a fool as many ways

as he could think of. It wasn't the children he was truly worried about; it was one young woman. Sara Beth Reese. She was the focus of most of his concern. He needed to stay out of trouble so he could continue to work on her behalf.

With a sigh and a nod, Taylor proceeded down the stairs. He was almost to the ground floor when he heard a commotion at the side door. One of the guards was scuffling with someone who seemed very determined to get inside.

The person was clad in a dark cloak. That alone made the hackles on the back of the doctor's neck rise. It was a warm, sunny afternoon. People were dressed for summer weather. So why would anyone wear a cape like that unless they were bent on skulking around and causing trouble?

He hurried to assist the guards. The hood fell back. Taylor's jaw dropped. "You!"

"I came to help," Sara Beth said, her cheeks rosy, her eyes bright.

"Help? You need to be locked up like your brother," Taylor said, making no attempt to hide his temper.

"Well, I'm here." She threw off the cloak and lifted her chin with obvious pride. "If you can't put me to work, then perhaps I should go back outside and see if I can assist someone else."

He took her arm, led her into an anteroom where

they could talk privately and closed the door. "Do you have any idea what you've walked into? Do you? There's about to be a lynching."

"I gathered as much when I passed the men rigging the nooses. It looked as if they were planning to hang two men."

"They are. Two murderers."

"Then what's the problem?"

Frustrated and so angry he could barely remain civil, Taylor stared at her. "The problem is that vigilante justice is frowned upon by the powers that be. Every one of these men can be arrested and tried for murder, and judging by the way this city has been run so far, they're likely to be convicted."

"Surely not all of them."

"Why not? And by being here, you're an accessory to their crimes."

He saw her green eyes widen with understanding as she looked at him. "Then so are you."

"Unfortunately, yes. I tried to talk them into waiting for martial law, but they wouldn't listen."

"What about your friend Mr. Coleman? Where's he?"

"Last I heard he was still trying to regain control of his former command. I don't hold out much hope for his success. He's too mild-mannered."

"What shall we do, then?"

Taylor threw up his hands and paced away from her. "How should I know? You're the one who thinks she has all the answers."

Sara Beth nodded. She had blundered into a terrible situation and had made things worse for Taylor—and for herself. So what should she do? What could either of them do?

"I came down the hill to take one last letter to the *Bulletin,*" she said. "Suppose you and I go try to deliver it? That way we'll surely have witnesses that we weren't directly involved with the hangings and you'll still be close enough to render aid if any of your friends are hurt."

She could tell by the expression on his handsome face that he was at least considering her idea. When he finally agreed, she was both relieved and thrilled. He had listened to her. He truly *did* value her opinion!

"I think I saw Tom King at the rear of the crowd directly across the street," Taylor said. "If we sneak out the back and circle around, we may be able to locate him without too much difficulty."

"And he'll swear that you and I are innocent bystanders," she added, encouraged.

"Hopefully. I don't know him as well as I knew his brother, but judging by the editorials he's been writing, he's sympathetic to our cause."

"I thought so, too. That's why I decided to write

one last letter and see if I couldn't get him to speak out on my behalf. You can understand that, can't you?"

Taylor nodded slowly, pensively. "Yes. It's your timing I take exception to, not your lofty goals."

"I need to get my cloak before we go," Sara Beth said, starting for the door.

He touched her arm and stopped her. "What am I going to do with you?"

"Accept me as I am?" she said with a slight smile.

Sighing, he opened his arms and welcomed her into his embrace, holding her as if he never intended to let go.

She was thrilled. And sad. And carefree, all at the same time. In his arms was where she found more solace, more peace and more joy than anywhere else. His presence fulfilled her, uplifted her spirits beyond imagining. Given a choice, she would gladly have stood in the doctor's embrace ad infinitum.

Finally he released her, set her away and said, "I'm sorry. I shouldn't have done that."

"Yes, you should," she insisted. "Whether you like it or not, you and I are part of each other's lives. We belong together."

"Don't be ridiculous. You're just confused because I've been trying to help you. We may be friends but there is nothing more to our relationship."

Soberly, Sara Beth shook her head. "I'm sorry to hear you say that, Taylor, because I've fallen in love with you and I don't have the slightest idea how to overcome those feelings and go back to the way things used to be before we met. Do you?"

Instead of insisting that she was wrong, he moaned and put his arms around her once again. She tilted her head back and raised her face to his.

Other young men had tried to steal a kiss in the past, but she had always managed to thwart their efforts. This time, however, she was more than ready to accept whatever Taylor chose to do. Yes, it was inappropriate. And, yes, she might be sorry later. But right now, right here, there was nothing she wanted more.

His breath was warm on her face. She closed her eyes.

And, wonder of wonders, he did kiss her.

You're a fool, he told himself. Yet there seemed to be nothing he could do to stop the way he felt, the way he was acting. In any other situation he would have been in total control, but not where Sara Beth Reese was concerned. She was the dearest person in his life and it was time she knew it, even though there was no chance they would be able to attain marital bliss.

The way she melted in his arms was nothing compared to the sweetness of her kiss or the surety he had that she was far from experienced in such things. That was enough to cause him to push her away, although he did keep hold of her hands.

"I should not have done that, Miss Reese. Please forgive me."

"No. I will not," she said, beginning to smile. "There is nothing to forgive. I was as much a party to what just happened as you were."

"I can tell that you do not make a practice of letting a man kiss you."

"Does that make a difference?"

"Yes," Taylor said solemnly. "It makes a great deal of difference. I would never do anything that might harm your reputation."

"Then I guess you will have to marry me," she said lightly.

"That's impossible."

"Why? I may not be as worldly as you are, but I sense that you care for me as much as I care for you. What is the problem?"

He released her, wheeled and paced away. "It's not that simple. You have no idea."

"Then enlighten me. Please?"

"I'm not ready to marry. And there's your family to consider." The moment those words were out of his mouth he was certain he had erred. "Your brothers, I mean."

Watching her expression change and harden, he knew she was hurt. Until she spoke, however, he wasn't sure why.

"My brothers? I think not. You cannot bear to risk your reputation by choosing the daughter of a man who is suspected of theft. You don't believe my father is innocent and you're worried that his supposed sins will reflect badly on you."

"Don't be ridiculous."

"Ridiculous? Hardly," she said with a catch in her voice. "I have seen how these things work. You want a wife who can bring honor and prestige to your name and your medical practice. Someone whose family can bolster your standing in San Francisco society and see to it that you draw the richest patients."

"I don't believe you're saying that." Taylor stared at her, his jaw agape. "Don't I volunteer at the orphanage?"

"Yes, and its rich patrons are exactly the kind of women whose influence will assist you in climbing the social ladder."

She wheeled and walked briskly toward the door.

"I'm going to get my cloak and then go looking for Tom King. Are you coming or not?"

Taylor was so shocked he almost couldn't make his feet move. She was so wrong about him that it was almost comical. He did not aspire to that kind of life, nor was he giving of his time and expertise to gain influence among the supporters of the orphanage.

Or was he? That notion brought him instant anguish. If there was even a slight chance that Sara Beth was right, he'd have to rethink his motives until he was certain they were pure.

In the meantime, he had to follow her no matter what she thought. She needed him. It was as simple as that.

Chapter Fourteen

Sara Beth was fighting to focus through her unshed tears. "I will not cry. I will not cry," she insisted under her breath. The press of the crowd helped distract her. She didn't know whether she was angry or sad or both. One thing was certain. She had been sorely disappointed in the one person she'd admired above all others.

Reaching the opposite side of Clay Street, she suddenly realized that she hadn't any idea what Tom King looked like. She would have recognized his brother in an instant, but unless the younger man was the spitting image of James there was no way she could be sure which of the nearby men he might be.

Taylor arrived moments later.

"Do you see him?" she asked, taking great pains to avoid actually looking at the doctor.

"I think so. Follow me."

As they weaved their way through the mass of people, Sara Beth let Taylor take the lead and shoulder a path, almost making the error of instinctively grabbing his hand to keep from being separated from him.

What a mistake that would be! The man already believed she was pursuing him and had made it crystal clear that he was not interested in her tender feelings. The last thing she wanted to do was to appear emotionally needy.

A roar was building. The crowd cheered. One quick glance told her that the first of the prisoners had just been hanged. He kicked for a few seconds before his body went limp.

Bitter gorge rose in Sara Beth's throat. How could she have ever imagined that she'd want to witness such a horrid spectacle? A life had ended. The crowd should be mourning the possible loss of the killer's eternal soul, not celebrating his death.

Taylor's voice drew her back to the task at hand. "This is Tom King," he said. "Tom, I'd like you to meet Miss Reese. She was acquainted with your late brother."

Looking up at the taller man, Sara Beth was surprised at how young he seemed. She smiled as he tipped his hat. "How do you do, Mr. King?"

"Fine, thank you. Especially now," the slim, sharply-dressed editor said, inclining his head toward the scene of the execution. "How may I help you, Miss Reese?"

She produced the letter she had written and solemnly handed it to him. "This will explain everything. Your brother had already broached the subject of the troubles connected with my home and family before his passing. I trust you will see how my dilemma coincides with the articles you have printed of late."

"Indeed?"

"Yes. If you have any questions, feel free to call upon me. I'm staying at the Ladies' Protection and Relief Society home on Franklin Street."

The editor touched the brim of his hat with the folded letter. "I look forward to reading this," he said.

Before she could respond, Taylor interrupted. "Don't print your source, whatever you do."

With a snort, Tom King shook his head. "No promises. I will write whatever seems best for my paper and for San Francisco."

Sobering, Sara Beth laid her hand lightly on the man's sleeve. "Do what you must. There are already evil forces set against me. God will be my refuge."

"I trust He will," King answered. "If you're staying in town to watch the rest of this spectacle, perhaps we can talk more later."

"Sorry, no," she said firmly. "I'm not needed here and I have chores waiting at the orphanage." Although that was not exactly true, she hoped the Lord would forgive her exaggeration. There were always jobs that needed doing at the home and she was adept at most of them. There would be plenty to keep her occupied. And by leaving, she would no longer have to face Taylor Hayward and see the rejection in his expression.

The way she viewed her situation, the less she had to do with the doctor from now on, the better.

In her deepest heart, however, she felt as if she herself had just died. Her spirit certainly had.

There was nothing more that Taylor could say. He'd already said far too much, and in the wrong way. The best thing to do at this point, he reasoned, was to let Sara Beth cool off before he tried to explain further.

"Do you want me to see you home?" he asked as they elbowed their way to the fringes of the throng.

"That will not be necessary." Her chin jutted out and her lips were pressed into a thin line. "I managed to get here by myself. I can get home as well."

"I'd offer to drive you, but my buggy is at the livery. I was afraid the horse might spook if there was a lot of shooting."

"Do you think there will be?"

"Probably not now. Later, if the army tries to capture our headquarters, perhaps. That was why I didn't want you to be there."

"Of course." Her voice was flat, almost expressionless, as if she was merely reciting words rather than feeling them.

"How will I know you're safe if I don't come along?"

"Suit yourself," Sara Beth said. "If you believe you need to establish further proof that you were not involved in the lynching, then accompany me. I'm sure Mrs. McNeil will gladly vouch for your integrity."

Taylor opened his mouth to refute her opinion of him, then closed it without speaking. When Sara Beth was in a mood like this there was little chance she'd be swayed by any explanation. Not that he knew what he should ultimately say. If he became too apologetic, she might think it was because he actually did want to court her. If he was too matter-of-fact, she'd assume he wasn't fond of her at all.

Sadly, that would be a blatant untruth. He did care. More than he could put into words. And he did want to marry her despite everything. It was only for her sake and the sake of her brothers that he would hold his tongue and encourage her to look for a husband who was more able to give her the finer things in life, like a home and expensive clothes and maybe even her own town buggy. That was the kind of easy life Sara Beth deserved. The life of a lady.

Sighing, he stayed several paces behind as he followed her. The sway of her cape hid her from view, but his imagination still saw her as clearly as ever. Her reddish hair was silky as a kitten's fur, her complexion clear and fair, her eyes bright like precious emeralds. The dusting of freckles across the bridge of her nose was icing on the cake. She was, she was… *Perfect,* his thoughts insisted. Taylor didn't argue. He knew it was true.

Okay, I love her, he finally admitted. *And she hates me because she thinks I'm ashamed of her family.* If she continued to believe that, perhaps she'd be more likely to seek a more suitable husband.

That notion stuck in his throat and left a bad taste in his mouth. Unless he or Sara Beth Reese left San Francisco and went somewhere where they'd never encounter each other again, he was liable to spend the rest of his life in agony. Every time they accidentally met on the street or, heaven forbid, she came to him for medical treatment, he'd suffer this sense of loss all over again.

There was only one honorable thing to do, one course to plot for himself. As soon as her estate was properly settled he'd board a steamer—any steamer—and leave the city.

Where he would go was unimportant. Escaping was the only way to cope. His heart insisted.

It wasn't the trudge up the hill that had tired Sara Beth so much. It was the knowledge that Taylor Hayward had remained so close by the whole time—near enough to turn and touch.

She didn't do so, of course. She had her pride. And she had grown so weary of doing battle with her emotions she'd simply shut them down as best she could. That had left her worn and weary and dreadfully demoralized but it had still been better than weeping and throwing herself at the poor man the way she'd yearned to.

Unfortunately, now that he had taken his leave, she couldn't seem to concentrate enough to complete any task. Clara had gotten so frustrated with her that she'd sent her out of the kitchen and told her to sweep the porches. Even that seemed beyond Sara Beth's current capabilities. When she had turned to admire her efforts she had realized what a poor job she'd done.

"I can't even wield a broom anymore," she muttered, thoroughly disgusted with herself. "I hope my talent with a pen is better than my household skills these days."

She'd wanted to linger downtown until the new editor had had a chance to look over her letter. If the doctor had not insisted on standing right there, she might have done so. However, since she'd had to struggle so hard to control her emotions in his presence, she had decided that heading home was the wisest choice. At least that way if she lost control and burst into tears, she'd be doing it where no one could see her suffering. Especially not Taylor.

Plopping into a chair on the porch, she released a sigh and waited for the tears to start flowing. They did not. Instead of weeping as she had expected, she simply felt empty, as if all her emotions had vanished into the fog that was now rising up from the bay. Soon the lush gardens would be shrouded in mist and the setting sun would be hidden. That kind of weather was the main reason why San Francisco remained so temperate year-round, and it suited her current mood perfectly.

Sara Beth felt as colorless as the dreary day, as cold as the fog in winter, as bereft as the mournful cries of the gulls. At this moment, she didn't care about anything. Not herself, not her stolen estate, not anything. Her heart was as icy as the wind that was rising off the sea and chilling her to the bone.

Shivering, she wrapped her arms around herself and went back inside, determined to think about something uplifting. To seek out company.

The first person who came to mind was baby Josiah. She had made it a point to visit with him in the nursery as often as possible and show him plenty of love. In another year he'd be old enough to join the other boys in the regular wards and then it would be much easier for her to keep track of his welfare.

In another year? Sara Beth shivered. Would she still be living here then? Most likely. And although Mathias could also remain there with her, it would be past the time when Luke had to leave because he was too old. Poor Luke. What would become of him? How would he survive on the streets? And how, dear Lord, was she going to see that he grew into a fine man like Papa Robert?

Seeking solace, she decided to gather all her brothers and talk to them. The older ones would be comforted by her efforts on behalf of the family.

And having them all together would be a mutual morale boost. At least she hoped it would.

"Are you sure the Reese boy understands what to do?" Bein asked. "We have to hurry. I'm expecting to be arrested any moment and once that happens I may not be able to pay you—or your men—easily."

Scannell nodded. "It's all set. When we get his signal it means he's ready to open the door and let one of his so-called friends inside."

"There won't be any slipups? You're certain?"

"Positive. I arranged for him to get involved with a local gang that listens to me. He trusts them."

"Are they old enough to carry out your orders?"

"The young man I'm sending is. I have plenty on him already. He'll do whatever I say because he knows he'll rot in jail if he fails."

"Even murder?" Bein was smirking.

"It won't be his first killing," Scannell replied with a wry chuckle. "That's why I know he'll cooperate."

"All right. Then get it over with so I don't have to worry about that irksome girl stirring up more trouble. I can handle everything else, just as I've planned, as long as there are no witnesses to testify against me."

"What about Harazthy?"

"I plan to sacrifice him under the wheels of the ore wagon, so to speak. After all, he's in charge of the mint operations and the late, lamented Robert Reese was his chief assayer. They can both take the blame."

Bein paused and cursed under his breath. "I don't care what I have to do. I am *not* going to prison."

Taylor was surprised to find that the crowds had dispersed quickly after the hangings. He had expected more celebrating and violence. Down by the docks there was a rowdy atmosphere, of course, but that was normal.

He decided to end his usual evening patient rounds at Abe Warner's Cobweb Palace. He didn't often frequent that place, or any like it. It was information in the form of gossip that he sought and he was not disappointed.

"Yup, I heard plenty," Abe said, grinning behind his silvery beard and mustache. "That Vigilance Committee is sure kickin' up its heels."

"I meant about the Reese family," Taylor said. "What's the word on the street regarding the investigation of theft from the mint?"

"Not much is new." The old man tilted his trademark top hat back by poking the brim with one gnarled finger. "Government men are all over the city, snoopin' into things that don't concern 'em. You know how it is."

"I'm afraid I do. Have they found any evidence besides those bits of scrap gold that were discovered at Reese's place?"

"I'm thinkin' yes. Leastwise, that's how it looks to me. Last I heard, they were fixin' to arrest his partner."

That news made Taylor's heart race and his breathing quicken. He grabbed the old man's forearm. "William Bein? The man who's trying to steal Sara Beth's house?"

Abe chuckled and winked at his companion. "The very same. Now, suppose you tell me a few things."

"Such as?" Taylor didn't like the twinkle in the old man's eyes or the lift of his mouth, especially since he assumed the amusement was a result of his questions.

"Such as, since when does a gentleman like you call a lady by her first name? What's been goin' on up at that orphanage, anyways?"

"Nothing illicit or immoral," the doctor answered soberly. "I have, however, become far too attached to Miss Reese."

"You could do worse. She's a mite comely little thing. Smart, too."

"I know."

"Then why the long face? She turn you down?"

"No. There was no proposal to turn down. I've told her she'd be wise to find a suitable swain and marry well, for the sake of her brothers and her estate."

"That why you're so all-fired determined to get that house back for her?"

"That's part of it, yes. The property is rightfully theirs and Bein's claim to it is not honorable, even if it may be legal."

"That still don't explain why you ain't interested in courtin' her. Does she like you?"

"Apparently. We get along fine. That's not the problem. There's simply no way a man in my position can adequately provide for her and her brothers." He made a derisive noise in his throat. "I'm lucky to collect enough fees to keep my office rent paid, let alone establish a home and start a family."

"You tell her that, did you?"

"Yes. Of course."

"In so many words?"

Taylor shrugged and arched his eyebrows. "I don't recall exactly what I said. I do know that she mistakenly assumed I was hesitant because of her father's tarnished reputation."

"Were you?"

"Of course not! I hadn't even considered that until she got upset and brought it up."

Abe began to laugh. "Sounds to me like a couple of children squabbling over a toy."

"I hardly consider affairs of the heart to be childish," Taylor countered. "I truly do care for her. I just refuse to saddle her with a husband who cannot properly provide for her and her family."

Sobering and getting a wistful look in his rheumy old eyes, Abe sighed audibly. "I had a gal once. A pretty one she was, too. Man, could she cook."

"I didn't know you'd ever been married."

"I haven't. That's what I'm tryin' to tell you. I wanted to sow my wild oats before I settled down, so I put to sea for a couple of years. When I came back, she'd got tired of waitin' and married another man." He gestured at the cluttered, crowded saloon. "Since then, it's been just me and this place and my menagerie."

"Surely you've had other opportunities to find a wife. This city has far more men than women, but still…"

"Never wanted any other gal," Abe said flatly. "Once you've tasted a rare steak, you don't want to settle for a pot of cold mush."

That analogy struck Taylor funny. He chuckled. "Believe me, I'm simply trying to do what's best for Miss Reese and her family."

"Then tell her so and let her make up her own mind. Because if you don't, you may never find another woman who takes your fancy the way that one has."

In his heart, Taylor knew Abe was right. His conscience, however, put up such a strong fight that he was at a loss as to which course to take.

Finally, he left the Cobweb Palace and stood on the boardwalk outside, listening to the foghorns in the distance and peering, unseeing, into the mist that was rolling in off the bay like waves of seawater at high tide.

The musty salt air smelled of all the sundry things that made the wharf a successful business enterprise, including the garbage from numerous restaurants and the offal from the fishing boats moored nearby.

There was blurred movement within the mist from time to time. Groups of men talked or laughed or cursed as they passed by. Some revelers were already so drunk they could hardly stand. Others were sneaking around as if waiting to lift purses from hapless sots and pitch their victims off the docks into the drink if they dared resist.

Taylor huffed. Half his patients would be suffering from combat wounds or hangovers after this weekend, not to mention the dangerous days to come. The worst was not over. Until the official law became trustworthy, no one would really be safe.

Suddenly, all he could think about was seeing Sara Beth again. Making sure she was all right. Telling her how he truly felt.

And if he bared his soul and she rejected him? Then he would consider her choice to be directed by the Heavenly Father they both worshipped and would stop dreaming of a happy time when they could be together.

Could he end those dreams by sheer force of will? He doubted it. Oh, he might be able to bid her a polite farewell and walk away, but his heart would be as scarred for life as old Abe Warner's.

Taylor realized he was as smitten as a schoolboy with his first crush and as committed as an old man who had spent a lifetime devoted to the same woman. If he and Sara Beth did not somehow find the path to marital bliss, he did not know how he would survive. The more he thought about her, the more he came to realize that she was the only one for him.

He didn't know how he could possibly toil any harder than he already was, but he would find a way.

He'd scrimp and save and hoard every spare penny until he was able to offer her a real home.

Would she wait? he wondered. Abe's beloved had not done so, yet perhaps that was because Abe had gone to sea. Taylor intended to stay right here where he could keep an eye on Sara Beth. Keep her safe.

Pondering such things, he shivered and started to walk briskly toward Franklin Street. The urge to see and talk to her—to confess his love—was so intense, so demanding, he almost broke into a run.

Chapter Fifteen

The temblor began as Sara Beth was assembling her brothers in the otherwise empty parlor. It shook the sturdy house briefly, causing the teardrop crystal pendants on the kerosene lamp bases to sway in unison and the fringe on the silk piano scarf to ripple.

Already bouncing on Sara Beth's knees, Josiah paid the shaking no mind, but both Mathias and Luke looked to their sister.

"It's nothing," she assured them. "I can't count the number of earthquakes I've noticed in the nearly eighteen years I've lived around here. Pay it no mind."

She continued bouncing the two-year-old on her lap and grinning at him while the older boys sat on the floor at her feet. "What I wanted to talk about is our plans for the future."

To her delight, Mathias's eyes widened expectantly. Luke, however, started to frown.

"Hear me out, please," Sara Beth said firmly. "I have been writing to the newspapers in the hopes their editorials will embarrass Uncle William enough to make him do right by us."

"He'd help us if you'd ask him nice and polite," Luke muttered.

"No. He would not." Sara Beth concentrated on her oldest brother while speaking to include them all. "William Bein has laid claim to Papa Robert's estate by virtue of their business partnership and refuses to listen to reason. He wants it all. He has told me this directly to my face."

Tears glistened in Mathias's eyes. She reached down to pat him on the head. "Don't worry, darling. As long as we have each other, we'll be fine. And I promise I'll keep us all together, somehow, no matter what I have to do."

"That's okay for you," Luke countered in a squeaky, breaking voice. "I'm the one who's gonna be pitched out into the streets any minute."

"We can work something out to stop that from happening. I know we can," she insisted. "All I'm asking is that you boys be patient and give me a chance. Mrs. McNeil has allowed us all to stay in spite of the rules against keeping boys once they've reached Luke's age. I don't really qualify either, since I'm not your mama."

"See?" Luke looked as if he was about to cry.

"Don't fret. I know she's not going to make us do anything else for a while."

"Yeah, right." Sniffling, the eleven-year-old scrambled to his feet and stormed out of the room.

Sara Beth chose to let him go and concentrate on her other siblings. She hugged the toddler close. "Don't worry about him, boys. Luke is just having trouble adjusting to living here. He'll get better as time passes."

At least, I hope he will, she added to herself. Luke's attitude troubled her greatly. He had always been the willing one, the sensible brother. Mathias had been the imp. And Josiah? He was his usual, cheerful, cherubic self, ever ready to grin and always eager to be held and babied.

That would change with age, of course. Luke had been a wonderfully sweet babe. So had Mathias, when he wasn't squalling for food or demanding more attention.

Thinking back on the boys' childhoods, she was struck that she had often played the part of their mother while Mama was busy with other chores. There had been times when it had seemed burdensome to do so, but in retrospect it had been for the best. She desperately needed her brothers to accept her authority.

Especially Luke.

Especially now.

Luke lit a candle and moved its flame across in front of the glass of a rear window. Then he waited.

The knock on the kitchen side door was so faint he would have missed hearing it if he had not been standing right there. His palms were clammy. He wiped first one, then the other on his pants before he held the candle high and reached for the latch.

"Who—who is it?"

"You know."

He did. And he was prepared to do anything he had to in order to fit in with the older boys who held his shaky future in their hands. There was nothing left for him but a life on the streets and he knew it.

Easing open the door, he admitted the shabbily dressed young man, noting as he passed that there was a foul, dank odor about him.

Everything stunk in his life, including his friends, Luke mused, disgusted. Papa had always preached honesty and Mama cleanliness and Godliness. What good had that done them?

"Where is everybody?" the interloper asked.

"Mostly in bed. My sister was in the parlor with my brothers last time I saw her so you should probably start in one of the other rooms."

"Start?"

"Stealing stuff," Luke said, frowning with puzzlement.

"Right. Stealing." He shrugged. "Forgot to bring a sack. Think you can scrounge me one? Pillowcases are good."

"Sure. Wait here. I'll be right back."

"Take your time," the would-be assassin said as the younger boy shielded the flickering candle with his cupped hand and left the kitchen. "Take all the time you need."

He inched closer to the hallway Luke had entered. He wasn't sure of the layout of the house, but he had a rough idea from talking to a few previous residents. That should suffice.

Pausing, he looked left, then right, letting his eyes adjust to the dimness. He'd begin where Luke had last seen his sister. And if she wasn't in the parlor, he'd come back to the kitchen and wait for her stupid brother to lead him straight to her. If luck was with him, he'd be finished and gone before anybody else even realized he'd been there.

He opened the small knife he had concealed in his hand and stepped forward.

* * *

Taylor had arrived on the grounds of the orphanage just as the moon was rising. Its reflection off the mist appeared to thicken the atmosphere until he could barely distinguish the house, let alone see well enough to tell what was going on inside.

He'd intended simply to knock on the front door and ask to speak with Sara Beth, but no lights continued to burn. That was a problem. Assuming the matron and her staff were already abed, his social call would seem quite odd.

Being thought inconsiderate was the last thing he wanted. If he hoped to eventually win over Sara Beth, he would need Mrs. McNeil's support as well as the goodwill of sensible matrons like Clara and Mattie. Rousing the household after all the lights were out was not the way to make a favorable impression.

Hesitating, he tried to decide how best to proceed. It wasn't that he believed that Sara Beth was in danger the way she had been earlier, he assured himself, yet there was a nagging insistence in the back of his mind that he must speak with her. *Tonight*. His mission would not wait till tomorrow. His heart would not let it.

The closer he got to the house, the more sinister and shadowy it appeared, giving him pause. That was an unnerving, totally abnormal reaction, particularly considering all the times he'd been summoned to the bedside of a sick child during the night and had responded to that call without a twinge of apprehension.

"Guess I'm a lot more overwrought than I thought," he whispered into the mist, mostly to hear his own voice.

"I'm also standing here babbling to myself," he added, beginning to smile and shake his head. "What would my patients think if they could see me now?"

That I'm praying, Taylor said, deciding easily that that was exactly what he should have been doing all along. When he momentarily closed his eyes and attempted to talk to God, all he was able to do was picture the love of his life and worry about her safety.

He managed a heartfelt, "Bless her and keep her, Father," before he gave up entirely and moved on.

Slowly circling the house, he kept an eye open for any indication that someone was still up. A lighted candle moved near one of the rear windows. Perhaps a child had taken sick and Sara Beth was fetching a dose of tonic?

The same candle cast a sliver of light into the swirling fog as the door was opened. A shadowy figure, not too large, passed in front of the flame and quickly slipped inside the building.

Taylor froze, his heart in his throat, his mouth suddenly dry. It wasn't the presence of someone at the door, or the fact that they were being admitted that bothered him. It was the stealth of movement and the obvious sense that one or more people did not want to be seen entering.

His pulse pounded in his temples. Sara Beth was inside that house. And now, so was someone who most likely did not belong there.

That was enough for him. He jogged up to the same portal, intending to demand admittance. He didn't have to. The door was not only unlocked, it stood ajar.

Taylor pushed it open and stepped inside.

The hair on the back of his neck prickled. Something was terribly wrong.

For Sara Beth, the evening had been nearly as tedious as the entire day. She was exhausted, yet she'd taken the time to walk Mathias back to his bed before returning sleepy Josiah to the nursery. Thankfully, both boys had behaved beautifully. She was not up to an argument after Luke's tantrum. What bothered her most was the chance that his bad attitude might influence Mathias.

Well, that couldn't be helped. Considering all the other boys who lived there, Luke's problems were truly insignificant. Not to him, of course, but given the rigors of surviving on the streets or going to bed hungry night after night, Luke had led a blessedly easy life. If only she could make him realize it.

"Father, help me," Sara Beth said as she lifted the kerosene lamp in one hand, her skirts in the other, and started up the staircase to bed.

A sudden shimmying of the pendants drew her attention to the lamp. The liquid fuel inside the glass base was trembling as if she had just shaken it. Only she had not.

She released her skirt and grabbed the banister for balance. There was a low, sustained rumble, as if the house was protesting being disturbed.

Waiting, she listened. In seconds, the noise of a few whimpering, frightened children was all she could hear. The earthquake was over quickly, as usual.

This spate of shaking had seemed harder and a bit more sustained, yet she doubted that there was anything to worry about. After all, the city experienced so many earthquakes that only the worst were even mentioned in the newspapers, and then only if there was no other interesting news to print that same day.

The last big temblor of any note had caused a few fires, however, so Sara Beth doused her lamp for safety. Better to eliminate the chance of a catastrophe than to accidentally drop the glass lamp and perhaps set the whole orphanage ablaze.

That thought gave her the shivers. So did being alone in the dark. Her vision adjusted slowly. She could discern little more than fuzzy shadows of the stairway and its newel posts. That was enough to allow her to proceed.

She took each step with caution, hiking a bit of skirt in the same hand as the dark lamp, leaving her other hand free to grasp the banister in case she lost her footing. The path up the stairs was as recognizable to her as the rest of the enormous house, yet she still took her time, slowly counting each step.

"Seventeen, eighteen, nineteen," she murmured, coming to the landing. Something made her pause there. Listen. Tense. "Luke? Is that you?"

Silence and darkness enveloped her. The atmosphere seemed suddenly dank, as if the whole house was in desperate need of airing. "Luke?"

When she held her breath and waited for a reply, she thought she heard someone else breathing. Panting. The stairs below her gave a familiar creak. Which riser always did that? Number four or five, if she remembered correctly. That meant that whoever was sneaking up behind her still had a ways to go. If she fled…

Whirling, Sara Beth raced up the last tier of the stairway as though she could see clearly. She tripped, regained her footing and continued. As soon as she reached the second floor she thrust the unlit lamp into a corner to keep it safe from an accidental spill, grabbed her skirt in both hands and ran for all she was worth.

She rushed past the rooms where others slept, thinking of sleeping innocents within. Instead of taking immediate refuge, she headed straight for the door leading to the old servants' quarters at the end of the hall. Her hand closed on the brass knob. It turned!

The narrow door gave with a noisy squeak of its hinges. "Unlocked. Thank You, God," she whispered, jerking it all the way open and pivoting through so she could slam and lock it behind her.

It wouldn't close tight! Sara Beth panicked and slammed it again. The bang of the wood smacking the door frame echoed hollowly, sounding muted as if…

A tug on her skirt told her all she needed to know. She eased her grip enough to extricate her clothing from the space and jerked the door closed again, just as someone crashed into it from the opposite side.

Sara Beth staggered. "No!" she screeched. "No."

Her heels were hard against the hidden stairway that led to the servants' quarters. She gripped the inside knob with both hands and pulled as hard as she could.

She felt the tarnished brass orb start to turn, then stop. Was she safe? Had it really been that easy?

Moments later she realized that whoever had been outside the door had ceased trying to gain entrance to her hiding place. Nevertheless, she continued to hold tight to the knob, waiting for another attempt.

None came. Quiet descended. All she could hear was the sound of her own heavy breathing and the pounding of her heart.

This was too easy. Too unbelievable. Perhaps her imagination had simply been working overtime and no one was actually out there. Or maybe Luke was playing a very unfunny joke to get even for whatever supposed slights she had committed.

She relaxed enough to press her ear to the door. "Luke? Is that you? Because if it is, I am not amused."

Someone chuckled. Someone whose voice was unfamiliar.

Although Sara Beth recoiled, she kept her hands on the knob. She didn't know how long her strength would prevail, but she was not going to let go and simply give a stranger the upper hand. No, sir. Not her. She had been through enough in the past weeks to prove her mettle, at least to her own satisfaction, and she was not a quitter.

On the other side of the door the soft, snide laughing continued. It would fade for a few seconds, then return. Something hard banged against the door, startling her.

"Please, God," she prayed aloud, "help me keep this closed."

"You won't have any trouble doing that," the voice in the hallway said. "Matter of fact, I'd like to see you try to open it."

It was a trick. It had to be.

"No way. Leave me alone."

"Gladly," her pursuer said. "I'm done here." He chortled with sinister glee. "Well, almost, anyways."

The voice sounded young to Sara Beth, perhaps a bit older than Luke, but not nearly as mature as Taylor. Meaning that she may have surprised one of the other boys, or a former resident, and he had merely reacted the way any misbehaving child might. He had tried to frighten her so she wouldn't tell Mrs. McNeil that he'd been prowling around at night when he shouldn't have been.

Beginning to catch her breath and calm down, she nevertheless delayed leaving the stairway alcove. It was dark as a tomb in there, yet comforting enough that she had no problem convincing herself to wait a little longer before venturing out. A few more minutes would suffice. And then she would do what was right, even if Luke had been involved in the prank. She would tell Ella everything.

She sighed. Poor Luke. Everything he did seemed to turn out badly. That was partly because of his disobedience, of course. That, and his hostile attitude. It was no wonder he hadn't made friends there the way she and Mathias had. Luke was not the kind of boon companion anyone would want— except perhaps one of the ruffians who hung around the wharf and begged for food or stole what he needed.

"That must never happen to Luke," Sara Beth told herself. "He deserves the kind of life he would have had if Papa and Mama were here."

Only they weren't. She was all the parent her brothers had left and she was sorely lacking, especially in matters of finances.

"Well, one problem at a time," she said, placing her hand on the knob and slowly starting to turn it.

The brass knob moved, as expected, but the door

did not budge. She tried again. Still it refused to open. She pushed her shoulder against it. The wood rattled, only giving a fraction of an inch.

Wide-eyed, Sara Beth stared into the blackness. It couldn't be locked, could it? She felt for a keyhole and found none. Therefore, there had to be another reason why she was apparently trapped in the stairwell.

Of course! That unusual banging noise she had heard would explain everything. Someone had crammed the wooden back of a chair from the hallway under the knob. That was what was interfering with the door's path.

She sank back on the lower steps and just sat there, thinking. If she raised a ruckus someone would surely hear, eventually, and rescue her. Shouting was a great idea—as long as her original pursuer was truly gone.

And as long as he was as innocent as she had imagined, she added. The notion that there might be real danger lurking in a place like this would never have occurred to her a few weeks ago. Now, however, she seemed to be seeing bogeymen behind every velvet drape and inside every ward.

"That is preposterous," Sara Beth insisted aloud. "Patently false. I am as safe here as I was in my own home."

Shivers shot up her spine when she pictured that home and the man who now laid claim to it. Panic began to well up within her and cause her to tremble.

She grabbed the knob and shook the barred door as hard as she could. It was only then that she realized there was more shaking going on than what she was causing. San Francisco was having another earthquake.

And this one was no trifle.

Chapter Sixteen

Taylor would have called out a greeting as he entered the orphanage if he hadn't been relatively certain mischief was afoot. Truth to tell, he hoped that that was all it was. Given the events of late, there was no telling what was actually going on inside the dark house.

He knew the floor plan by heart, making it easy for him to wend his way through the kitchen and check out the other rooms on the ground floor. Nothing seemed amiss until he rounded a corner into the hall and ran smack into someone.

Instinct made him grab for the smaller figure. "Whoa. Hold on. I'm not going to hurt you," Taylor assured him. "What's going on?"

"None of your business," the boy said, struggling to free himself.

Taylor was certain he recognized that voice. "Settle down, Luke. All I want to know is why you're up and about when everybody else seems to have gone to bed."

"Let me go."

"Not until you talk to me." He hesitated, bracing himself as he felt a tremor beneath his feet. "Did the earthquakes scare you? Is that it?"

"Uh, right."

"Where's your sister?"

"How should I know? It's not my job to take care of her."

Although Taylor couldn't see the boy's face as more than a shadow, he could hear the contempt in his tone. "You should be thankful she doesn't feel that way about you."

"I don't care. I can take care of myself."

With that, Luke gave a quick jerk and managed to twist out of Taylor's grip. In an instant he had ducked beneath the doctor's outstretched arms and fled.

Something white on the floor at his feet caught Taylor's attention. He bent and picked it up. It was an empty pillowcase.

Puzzlement quickly gave way to anger. Evidently, Luke had been planning to fill the linen bag with booty and then leave the orphanage, just as many unmanageable boys had done in the past. It took a special kind of person, a truly forgiving soul, to keep the doors of the home open to all those in need when so many took advantage of the kindness.

Troubled by his conclusions, Taylor sighed. He would have to inform the matron, of course, and then tell Sara Beth. Such painful honesty would probably do his personal cause little good, but he had no choice. If the boy was on the wrong path it was up to them all to try to turn him around.

He smiled slightly. His own youth had not exactly been misspent, but he had come close to making a few bad decisions, for which he would still be paying if a kindly church deacon had not befriended him. There was hope for Luke. Especially if they could keep him from taking that first step into a life of crime.

Fisting the pillowcase, Taylor started up the stairs. He would rouse some of the adults within the household and enlist their help in searching for Luke and trying to talk sense into him. Perhaps Mrs. McNeil would also notify Sara Beth. No matter what else occurred, Taylor was determined to follow through on his plans to speak with her. To ask her to consider him as a beau.

If he had been paying more attention to his path instead of musing about Sara Beth, he might have avoided a collision with another person galloping down the stairs.

The wiry youth crashed into Taylor's shoulder as he bolted past, almost knocking him off his feet.

"Hey! Watch out," the doctor shouted, wheeling and grabbing the banister.

The youth didn't slow. Nor did he answer except to curse colorfully. Taylor didn't recognize his voice or his stature, although there were a few residents who may have been nearly that tall. In the dark and on the stairway, it was hard to judge size accurately.

Pausing to stare after the fleeing figure, he had decided to return to the kitchen for a candle or a lamp when he noticed a faint glow coming from the upper story. Was someone else awake after all?

Light reflection moved and increased as he watched, beginning to shimmer on the walls and ceiling. It looked like the effects of a lamp, yet…

He sniffed as the air began to thicken. *Smoke?* His heart leaped. For a few seconds he was speechless.

Then, he recovered enough to begin to run up the stairs, two at a time.

His eyes burned and watered. The most important task was rousing the household and getting everyone out. He made a fist and started down the hall, banging on each bedroom door in turn and shouting, *"Fire!"*

* * *

Sara Beth had not wasted time pushing on the blocked door. Instead, she had followed the closed-in stairway with the hope of finding an alternate exit.

The abandoned servants' quarters at the top of the stairs were stuffy. One window at the end of the narrow attic room admitted just enough moonlight to allow her to see shadows and shapes in spite of the fog.

Arms extended, she cautiously worked her way around the room, sliding her feet along the dusty floor so she wouldn't trip. There was a table, a bedstead and a rickety ladder-back chair, which she found the hard way by almost falling over it. Other than that, the place seemed totally abandoned.

Thankfully, its small dimensions allowed her to quickly examine the wainscoted walls, looking for an exterior door. At this point she didn't care where it led as long as it eventually brought freedom.

The moment she touched the edge of the jamb and realized she'd found what she'd sought, she reacted with thankfulness. Unshed tears welled.

She kept repeating, "Praise the Lord," while her fingers explored the rectangular jamb. Like the entrance from which she had emerged, this portal was narrow and fitted with a brass knob.

She grabbed it. Twisted. Unfortunately, this door remained firmly in place. "No, no, no," she whispered. "Please, Jesus, let me get out."

Still exploring by touch, Sara Beth found that this door, unlike the one at the bottom of the stairs, did have a keyhole. To her dismay, however, there was no key in evidence.

Dropping onto her hands and knees she began to feel along the dusty floor, hoping against hope that a key had simply fallen out and was lying there waiting for her to pick it up. There was nothing but dirt.

Frustrated, she huffed in self-disgust. This was a fine kettle of fish, wasn't it? Morning might come before anyone missed her, let alone heard her cries for help and either located the right key with which to let her out or removed the chair from the door on the floor below.

"Well, at least if I can't get out, no one can get in this way to harm me," she told herself, starting to worry more about the others in the mansion, especially the innocent children, and realizing that there wasn't a thing she could do about it.

Looking for diversion, she edged carefully toward the narrow window and gazed at the city below. Normally, with the weather as foggy as this, she would not have been able to see much.

Her hand flew to her throat. Not only could she see plenty, she could tell that this most recent quake had done the same thing that had happened in the past. It had started fires.

She could only spot two places aglow through the thick, moist air, but there might be more. There probably were. And that meant that the volunteer fire brigades would be out in force, risking their own well-being while trying to save life and property.

Prayer was her only recourse, the only way she could hope to help. She folded her hands and closed her eyes. "Please, Father, help them. Help them all. And keep the firemen safe from harm, too."

Her prayer then expanded to include her friends and family, especially Taylor Hayward. He would undoubtedly be out and about, too, offering care and doing all he could to ease suffering. That was the kind of man he was. Stalwart. Sacrificing. Admirable beyond words.

"And I love him, Father," Sara Beth said aloud. "He's ashamed of my family but I can't help myself. I love him so much it hurts. I just don't know how to stop myself."

Opening her eyes, she caught a glimpse of white objects moving on the lawn below like tiny flower petals blowing in the wind. Nightshirts? Yes! Lots of them. Myriad children were scurrying around the expansive gardens and it looked as if plenty of adults were with them, shooing them hither and yon like gaggles of geese.

Had there been earthquake damage to this building, too? she wondered. It seemed sturdy enough to her. Then again, she wasn't privy to the whole structure.

It suddenly occurred to her that this had been the answer to her prayer for the children. As long as they were awake and in the company of their caretakers, they would be safer than sleeping in their beds with a stranger prowling the halls.

And, perhaps, when all the excitement from the shaking died down, someone would miss her and start a search.

She smiled. Maybe, since God was already answering her pleas, the person who came looking for her would be Taylor Hayward! There was no one she would rather it be. She could hardly wait.

"Where are the Reese boys?" the doctor shouted. "I don't see them."

Mrs. McNeil pointed. "Over there. With their ward caretakers. We got everybody out safely, thanks to you."

"What about the baby?"

"The people from the nursery are all out in the back garden. I'm sure he's fine."

"What about Sara Beth?"

The matron's eyes saucered. "I don't know. She must be here somewhere. She's probably helping with the littlest ones. I know the staff checked each ward carefully before leaving."

Taylor wasn't satisfied. Until he saw the love of his life with his own eyes, he was going to keep looking. The fire was still small enough that he could reenter the orphanage if he had to. And if he could not quickly locate Sara Beth, that was exactly what he was going to do.

Running, he rounded the corner by the kitchen and ran smack into Luke. "Where's your sister?"

The boy's expression was unreadable.

"Answer me." He shook Luke by the shoulders. "Tell me. Where is she?"

"I—I don't know."

"Where did you last see her?"

"In—in the parlor. I told you."

"That was half an hour ago. Have you seen her since?" He gave the boy another shake. "Well?"

Luke lowered his head until his mop of hair masked his face, but Taylor could tell plenty by his body language. The boy was clearly hiding something. And as long as Sara Beth was unaccounted for, he was not going to let him get away with any subterfuge.

"Look, son, I don't care what else you were up to tonight. Understand? I just want to make sure your sister is all right."

"Why?"

"Because I care about her—and so should you," Taylor said. "She's the glue that's holding your family together and she's risked her life to do it."

"Oh, really?"

"Really." Taylor would have liked to turn the boy over his knee and give him a proper education with a hickory switch the way a few of his teachers had enlightened him when he was a child, but he didn't have time to waste.

"So, what were you and your friend up to tonight?"

Luke cringed beneath the man's grasp. "I don't know what you're talking about."

"Yes, you do. Who was he and what were you two planning? I found the sack where you dropped it. Was he going to make you a member of his gang if you helped him rob this place?"

His head snapped up. "How did you know?"

"Because I was young and stupid once, too. And because I think I may have recognized the fellow who ran into me right after you did. I couldn't place him at first but now that I think about it—"

"We never took a thing," Luke insisted.

"Only because a fire started and you had to get out with everybody else."

Wide-eyed, the boy swiveled his neck and stared at the mansion. "Do you think Sara Beth…?"

There was a glow behind the front door and smoke was billowing from several open upstairs windows. Taylor figured the building was still salvageable, assuming one of the fire brigades arrived fairly soon.

"I don't know," Taylor said. "You go find Mathias and then both of you wait with Josiah. If she's in there, I'll find her."

"Let me go, too."

"And have to spend my time tracking you down again when you're already safe out here? No way. For once in your life, do as you're told."

Expecting an argument, Taylor was astounded when the teary-eyed boy merely nodded and said, "Yes, sir."

"Is she dead?"

"As good as." The assassin held out his hand. "Where's my money?"

"I expected you to use the loot from the orphanage to pay yourself," Bein said, laughing wryly.

"I had to leave in a hurry. I didn't get nothing."

"That's hardly my fault."

"If you don't pay me I'll—"

"You'll what? Talk? Blame me? I hardly think so. Not when the sheriff tells me you have another murder hanging over your head." He scowled. "Did you make sure she was dead?"

"She will be. I left her trapped in a closet and set the hall outside it on fire. She'll bake like a loaf of bread in an oven."

"She'd better. What about all the others in that big house? What if they die, too?"

"That's none of my concern," the assassin said. "I don't owe nobody there a thing. They turned me away after my ma died and my pa took off for the gold fields. Said I was too old."

"I hope you were old enough and smart enough to handle this job."

"I was." He brandished the knife that he'd intended to use on Sara Beth before his plans had changed. "Now, let's you and me talk about money."

Chapter Seventeen

The stuffiness of the tiny upper room was growing unbearable. Sara Beth tried to open the small window. It had apparently been closed for so long that it was stuck tight, because no matter how hard she strained it wouldn't budge.

She sighed, wishing she were down on the lawn in the fresh air with the children. Patience had never been one of her virtues, as she was being constantly reminded. She might have many pleasing traits such as kindness, forbearance, love, joy in adversity, forgiveness...

The instant she had that particular thought, she was penitent. She was not forgiving. Not the way the Good Book said she should be. She was holding a grudge against the man whom she believed had

had her parents killed and she didn't see any way to stop hating him for the horrible things he had done.

That was probably the key, she reasoned. It was all right to hate evil acts, but not to hate the person who carried them out. Sadly, she could not manage that either.

She immediately visualized William Bein. He may not have been directly responsible for Papa Robert's and Mama's deaths, but he had certainly taken advantage of them. And who was to say for certain that he had not been the evil force behind everything? Papa had visited the wharf that night to speak with someone he had caught cheating. Who fit that description better than dear old Uncle William?

Taking a deep breath and releasing it as a sigh, Sara Beth was surprised to catch a whiff of a strange, acrid odor. She frowned. In the dimness of the moonlit garret she couldn't spot any source of such a smell, yet…

She sniffed. Followed her nose. It took her to the stairwell she had climbed to gain access to the abandoned room. Continuing to inhale slowly, thoughtfully, she made up her mind.

Smoke. It was smoke she was smelling. It was drifting up the stairway and starting to infiltrate the tiny room. That was why all the children had been taken outside. The orphanage was on fire!

Heart pounding, she spun in a circle, trying to decide what to do. There was no way out that she could see. Her one best hope was probably staying as far from the flames as she could until someone rescued her.

"Only no one knows where I am," she lamented. "No one but God." Her eyes widened as she noted the smell of burning wood increasing.

One thing was certain. The same Heavenly Father who had given her a useful intellect would expect her to use it rather than simply sit there and become a victim of her own lack of initiative. But what could she do? And how long might it be before someone found her?

Determined to isolate herself from the acrid air as much as possible, she whipped off her petticoats and hurried down the stairs to stuff them at the base of the door. That would buy a little time. So would finding a source of breathable air.

It took her only a moment to decide to break out the stuck window. Grabbing the chair, she struck the glass with its ladder-shaped back. Once. Twice. Nothing happened.

Finally frantic enough to use her full strength, she managed to crack the heavy glass. It shattered in a starburst pattern that she was then able to break away from the frame. Leaning out, she took deep, cleansing breaths. Night air from the bay had never smelled better.

Now that there was nothing but open space between Sara Beth and the people on the lawn, she began to shout. "Help! Up here. I'm trapped!"

To her dismay, there was so much racket and mayhem going on below, no one even looked up.

She tried again and again. Nothing.

"Father, what shall I do?" she prayed, panicking. *The chair!* That was it. If she could throw it out the window, perhaps someone would figure out where it came from and send aid.

Hefting it once more, she tried to fit it through the narrow sash. It was no use. The window frame was at least three inches narrower than the seat of the old chair. And it was the smallest thing in the nearly empty room.

"What else? Think," she murmured, thoroughly frustrated and at a loss as to how to help herself. This was maddening. She felt like screaming, like kicking the wall, like smashing everything in sight.

"That's it!"

Reaching for the chair once again she drew back and swung it the way she would have a wire rug beater. It met the sturdy bed frame with a crack and started to splinter. Two more hard whacks and the back parted from the seat.

Sara Beth raced to the window. She could see a man-drawn fire wagon being tugged up the driveway by countless firemen and volunteers. Soon they would be in place to start battling the blaze.

But would they have it under control in time to save her life? She didn't know. All she could do at this point was start flinging parts of the broken chair out the window in the hopes that someone would notice.

That, and screech at the top of her lungs. Given the level of noise below, she knew her efforts in that regard would probably be futile. Nevertheless, she tried.

"Help! I'm up here. Look, somebody. Look at me!"

Taylor was back inside the building, searching from room to room the way he had before the fire had started. He couldn't take the chance that Sara Beth had made it downstairs, only to lose consciousness.

That thought chilled him to the bone. She had to be all right. She had to be. He couldn't lose her.

"Sara Beth," he shouted. "Where are you? Answer me."

Most of the smoke had stayed on the upper floors, the same way it rose up a chimney, and it lay like bay fog in a cloud that extended halfway to the landing on the main stairwell. If he was going to move toward that, he'd need to cover his mouth and nose.

Dashing to the kitchen, he whipped off his coat and shoved it into a pail of water that was awaiting the cooks. It wasn't much, but it would have to do, he reasoned, quickly soaking the jacket.

He pressed the wet wool cloth to his face like a mask and returned to the stairs. Sara Beth was obviously not on the ground floor. There was only one thing to do. He had to enter the fire zone to search. No other plan was acceptable.

The chair back was the first to go. It sailed out over the mansard roof and dropped out of sight. "Help," Sara Beth screeched. "Up here. Help!"

She followed with the spindle legs, then stomped on the seat to try to break it more. When it refused to crack, she upended it and heaved it out the window vertically. It was, unfortunately, so heavy that it didn't clear the edge of the roof.

Turning, hoping to find some other object she might have overlooked, she was stunned to see that there was now a lot of smoke rising from the stairwell. As it reached the main room it headed straight for the open window.

By breaking the glass she had evidently created an updraft that was going to suck the fire right to her!

As Taylor crested the stairs, he could tell that the fire's origin was at the far end of the hallway. Thankfully, it seemed confined to an area where there were no bedrooms so the children had been able to escape. If it had started mid-hallway instead, there would surely have been numerous victims trapped.

Peering at the blaze, he was taken by the fact that it seemed so isolated. There was really no fuel in that area other than the walls and floor, yet it was burning with a high, hot flame. The kind of flame that the oil from a dropped lamp might produce.

He paused for the length of a heartbeat to assess the situation. If the firemen didn't get water on this conflagration soon, it could easily claim the whole building. He lowered his wet coat and thought about trying to beat out the fire with it, then concluded that that effort would be futile.

An object within the flames caught his eye. It looked for all the world as if a fancy side chair had been placed in the middle of the inferno. Why in the world would a chair be parked in front of a door like that?

He racked his memory. Where did that door lead? He didn't recall ever opening it, yet it must have been of some use, at least in the days when the mansion had been a private home. He supposed it could be a closet, but if that were the case, then why prop a chair at such an awkward angle in front of it?

There was no way Taylor could find out without breaching the worst of the fire, and he was not about to do something so reckless.

His first instinct was to continue checking the bedrooms, but since Mrs. McNeil had assured him that that had already been done, perhaps he'd be wasting his time.

He hesitated, thinking, wondering, praying. If he wanted to ask about that strange door he was going to have to return to the lawn and find someone who knew. He didn't understand why the urge to do so was so compelling. He could not seem to shake it no matter how much he argued with himself.

"Sara Beth needs me," he kept insisting.

Yes, she does, his heart answered. *And if she's truly trapped behind that door, she may already be dead.*

That was more than Taylor could take. Giving no thought to his own well-being, he wrapped his wet coat around his forearm, held it up like a shield against the heat and charged at the burning chair.

The heat was intense. The flames singed his hair and eyebrows. He kicked the remains of the chair away with his boot and tried to grab the knob. It made his hand sizzle.

Shouting in agony, he sheathed his palm in a piece of the coat and tried to twist the handle once again. He was already nauseated by the pain. If he didn't get the door open this time he was going to have to give up or risk collapsing where he stood.

"What was that?" Coughing, Sara Beth strained to listen. By now, the crackle and roar of the fire was so loud she wasn't positive she'd actually heard a shout.

Nevertheless, she screamed again. "Help! Help me."

A mighty whoosh of air carried billowing smoke clouds up the stairway. *Oh, no!* The door must have burned away and now there was no barrier between her and the blaze.

She backed toward the window, wondering if it would be possible to squeeze through such a small opening. Probably not, she decided, although trying to do so was starting to look like her only chance of surviving.

The black smoke whirled. Eddied. Sara Beth's eyes burned. Her throat felt as though it was closing. She gasped and coughed so hard it doubled her over.

Suddenly, strong arms grabbed her and for an instant she wondered if she had died and was being taken to heaven in the arms of an angel. Then, she realized that her prayers had been answered in the best way. Taylor Hayward was beside her.

She threw her arms around his neck and held on for dear life.

"How did you get up here?" he asked, gasping and hacking worse than she was.

"Somebody was chasing me. They blocked the door."

"I saw. If he hadn't done it with a chair I might not have found you in time."

Her eyes were watering from the smoke and she was weeping with joy at the same time. "That other door," she said, pointing. "It's locked."

Taylor kept an arm around her as he shepherded her across the room. He didn't even pause to try the knob. He simply kicked the door with the sole of his boot and it sprang open.

In mere seconds they were on their way down an outside stairway and headed for the garden. Sara Beth was doubly thankful that he had not let go of her because she wasn't sure how steady she'd be if he did.

As far as she was concerned, if Taylor never left her side again it would be just fine with her.

Chapter Eighteen

They emerged into a small, secluded side garden that was hemmed on three sides by manicured hedges. There was plenty of shouting and other noise in the background, but they were temporarily alone.

Sara Beth faltered, coughing and gasping for breath as they made their way to a stone bench.

She sat first. Taylor plopped down beside her. He was also struggling to get enough air.

"The children…are they…safe?" she asked, wheezing.

He nodded. "Yes. The staff got them all out. Everybody was on the lawn, except you."

"How…how did you find me?"

He coughed again, then managed a smile. There

was moisture glistening in his eyes that she hoped was not simply an adverse reaction to the smoke.

"Divine providence again, I guess." He took her hand. "I was puzzled by that chair in front of the door in the hallway. There was just something about it that didn't look right. I don't know why I felt so strongly except that perhaps the Good Lord was guiding my thoughts."

"That sounds good to me," she replied. The tender, loving expression on his face touched her deeply. She reached across to caress his cheek and felt the coarseness of a beginning stubble. "You need a shave, Doctor."

"No," Taylor said as he covered her hand with his own. "What I need is you."

She was thunderstruck. Was he saying what she thought he was? Could it be? Nothing in her personal life had changed for the better. She was still responsible for her brothers and Papa Robert's reputation was still under a cloud.

"Close your pretty mouth," he said, starting to grin. "You're gaping at me."

"Little wonder. You aren't making sense. Did the fire unhinge you?"

"If that was what it took to wake us up to our true feelings for each other, then it was for the best. Whoever set that blaze did us a favor."

"He did?"

"Yes. He did," Taylor said as he enfolded her in his embrace. "I had come here tonight to explain myself and to beg you to forgive me. To grant me the chance to court you."

"I think it's already too late for that," Sara Beth said, leaning her cheek against his strong shoulder. She felt as if she could hear the rapid pounding of both their hearts. She could certainly feel the racing of her own.

"Then I suppose I shall have to do the right thing and ask for your hand in marriage," he said. "Since you lack parental guidance, perhaps Mrs. McNeil will suffice."

"Or old Abe Warner," Sara Beth offered. "I can just hear him laughing at the both of us over it."

Taylor sobered. "We will have to wait to actually marry, of course."

Her brow furrowed and she leaned away to look at his face. "Why?"

"Because I can't properly provide for you and your family yet. I promise I'll do my best to save for the day when I can."

"Oh." The joy of his proposal remained. The excitement of becoming his bride, however, quickly faded. "I suppose that is sensible."

"Very."

"It's also too bad. I really do want to leave this place and have a real home again." The moment she'd spoken she realized that he might misunderstand.

"Is that why you're agreeing to marry me?"

"No. Of course not. No more than you were hesitant to ask because of my father's reputation. I can see that now. We've both been trying so hard to behave properly in a difficult situation that we've lost sight of how we feel about each other. That's the most important thing."

Pausing and gazing into his eyes, she swallowed hard before she added, "I love you, Taylor. I have for ages."

This time, there was no doubt in Sara Beth's mind that he was touched. When he said, "I love you, too," his eyes glistened with unshed tears and there was so much affection in his expression that it stole her breath and made her giddy.

Sara Beth suddenly understood that this was the kind of overwhelming love and devotion Mama had found with Papa Robert, the kind that had made her follow him to the wharf and willingly sacrifice her life to try to save his.

And she could finally forgive her mother for leaving her family the way she had. It was a shock to realize that she had blamed her parents for the decisions that had ended their lives so early. But she had. And that had led her to question God, as well.

Yet here she sat, looking forward to the future and a whole new life with Taylor Hayward. Who knew? Perhaps she would continue to learn medicine at his side and someday fulfill that dream, too.

The way she saw it, at this point in her life, the future held nothing but possibilities and opportunities.

Cuddling closer, she closed her eyes and thanked her Heavenly Father for bringing her and her loved ones through the fire. Literally.

Taylor soon led Sara Beth back to the front lawn and reunited her with Mrs. McNeil, then wrapped a loose bandage around his burned hand before he went to fetch the boys. He intended to suggest that they welcome their sister and celebrate survival with her. To his relief and delight, even Luke seemed amenable to the idea.

"Is she okay?" the eleven-year-old asked. He and Mathias were tagging along while Taylor carried Josiah.

"She breathed a lot of smoke, but she'll be fine."

"Are you okay?" The boy was eyeing his bandaged hand.

"Yes. It's not as bad as it looks."

"How did the fire start?"

"How?" Taylor gave him a withering glance and stayed stern in spite of the obvious fact that the boy was worried. "Suppose you tell me."

"I didn't do it!"

"No, but I suspect your friend did. What happened to him, anyway? Where did he go? I haven't seen him since he crashed into me on the stairs. That was just about the time I first saw the flames."

"Why would he do that?"

"I don't know. Maybe he was supposed to."

"That doesn't make any sense," Luke argued. "If the house was on fire he wouldn't have time…"

"Right. To steal anything. I had that part already figured out, assuming that was his goal. Where did you meet him, anyway?"

"Down by the docks. You saw."

"*That's* where I remember him from. You're right. I did see you two together." He hesitated, mulling over what he knew. "That gang of rowdies just came up to you and took you in? Is that what you're telling me?"

"Yes. So?"

"So, it doesn't make sense unless they knew who you were and where you were living."

"They wanted to rob the orphanage?"

Taylor was slowly shaking his head. "I thought

so at first, but now I'm not so sure. Think back. When you met them, did they ask you anything about your family, your sister in particular?"

Judging by the way the color drained out of the boy's face, Taylor assumed he was onto something. "They did, didn't they? What did they want to know?"

"Nothing much. Just what her name was and where she was staying. I thought they were worried that my parents would wonder where I was and wanted to make sure I didn't have any."

"Did they ask about your brothers? The rest of your family?"

Luke was trembling and wide-eyed when he answered, "No."

Firemen had not been able to draft through their hand pumper at the orphanage the way they did from the city's cisterns, so they had formed a bucket brigade to keep the reservoir full. They were already manning the hose and getting the worst of the fire under control by the time Sara Beth saw Taylor returning with the boys.

She opened her arms to Josiah and was a bit chagrined when he recoiled.

"I think you and I are too dirty and smoky for his taste," Taylor explained. "He wasn't thrilled when I picked him up, either."

"Of course." She grimaced at her sooty hands and used the back of her wrist to push loose hair off her forehead. "I must look a fright."

The doctor laughed. "You are the most beautiful sight I have ever seen, Miss Sara Beth."

"And you are prejudiced."

"Decidedly so." Passing Josiah to Mrs. McNeil, he grinned. "I suppose I should speak my piece since there will probably never be a better time."

She glanced briefly toward her elder brothers. They were standing back as if they sensed something significant was about to happen. "You haven't thought about all this and changed your mind, have you? It is a lot to take on."

"I would adopt a hundred children if it pleased you," Taylor said, continuing to grin widely. He turned to the matron. "Mrs. McNeil, it is my desire to have this young lady's hand in marriage. May I have your blessing?"

Giggling, Ella blushed and nearly jumped up and down with glee. Sara Beth suspected she might have done so if she had not been toting Josiah on her hip. "Mercy sakes, yes. I thought you two young people would never see the light. I was running out of ways to throw you together."

Stepping closer to Taylor, Sara Beth was not at all

surprised to feel his arm encircle her shoulders once again. This was life as it should be, she mused. All else paled in comparison to her feelings for her beloved.

The way she saw the situation, there was only one more obstacle to their happiness. They needed to clear her stepfather's name and regain possession of the house on Pike Street. Taylor might not have thought of it yet, but that building was the perfect location. She would use the house for business as she had once planned, only it would not house a millinery, it would become a doctor's office. Taylor Hayward's office.

She began to smile. Let him try to postpone their wedding then.

The *Bulletin* printed a string of revealing articles over the course of the next few months that led to a rapid shakeup in San Francisco politics.

Taylor had been initially worried about repercussions, but by July the Vigilance Committee had hanged several more miscreants and had driven Chief Justice Terry out of town. Then they had quietly disbanded. General Sherman had resigned in frustration and had been replaced by General Volney Hayes, a lawyer and former member of congress from Texas, so things were finally getting back to normal.

It was Taylor's pleasure to bring news of William Bein's arrest for embezzlement. He found Sara Beth in the kitchen garden, digging onions.

"Hello there."

Grinning, she whirled and dusted off her hands. "Taylor! I'm so glad to see you. If I had known you were coming I would have washed up and put on a pretty frock."

"You look beautiful to me," he said, ignoring the dirt and taking her hands. "I brought news."

"What?"

"Your nemesis has been arrested for robbing the U.S. Mint. The investigators watched him till they caught him red-handed. He even admitted the theft."

"Really? Oh, my. What about Papa Robert? Did Bein's confession clear him?"

"It looks like it may. According to Tom King, the United States Grand Jury is planning to indict their boss, Augustin Harazthy. Once that happens, the whole truth should come out."

The look of relief on her face was so immeasurable he didn't know what else to say. Instead of more words, he decided to let his actions speak for him.

Tilting her chin up with one finger, he placed a gentle kiss on the lips he had yearned to kiss again for literally months. When she melted against him, he was astounded by how perfect she was. How lovely. How dear.

He stepped back, staggered by the effect of that one simple kiss.

Sara Beth's eyes held a dreamy look and her lips began to lift in the whisper of a smile. She sighed before she said, "I thought you would never get around to doing that again." The smile spread to include her eyes, her rosy cheeks. "It was even better than the first time."

"Perhaps you're learning," Taylor teased.

"Or you are," she countered, laughing. "Let's just promise to keep practicing till we're sure it's perfect."

"You are already so perfect it takes my breath away," he confessed. "I don't know how much longer I can continue to be the kind of gentleman you deserve."

"Then I suggest you stop stalling and marry me," Sara Beth said boldly. She took him by the hand. "Come. I have something special to show you."

Although he knew he wasn't financially ready to take a bride, he also knew it was not fair to Sara Beth to keep delaying. She was a good woman. She deserved a proper wedding and a suitable home. He had saved some money but not nearly enough to set up housekeeping. What could he do? What should he do?

She led him into the kitchen and pointed to the table. "Sit there."

"Yes, ma'am," he said, much to Clara's—and Sara Beth's—obvious amusement.

"I had not heard about William Bein's arrest, but I did receive an official document from the court this morning." She reached into her apron pocket and unfolded a piece of paper. "It says that the title to the family house and property is mine."

Taylor started to rise, intending to give her a congratulatory hug. She stopped him with an upraised hand. "Wait. There's more."

"More? What else was there?"

"Just this," she said as she reached into a cupboard beneath the sink and pulled out a slab of wood. "I had it made from the mahogany that was salvaged from the upstairs hall after the fire. I couldn't think of a better source, and I wanted it as a memento, too."

Flipping the board around, she proudly displayed it.

Taylor was afraid he was going to disgrace himself by weeping. He blinked as he struggled to control his emotions. It was a new shingle. A sign that declared, "Doctor Taylor Hayward" in gilt letters. Below that was the address on Pike Street.

It took him several seconds to see what she was getting at. "How could you have known to do that?"

"I didn't," Sara Beth said. "It was just a dream I had and I figured it was best to act as if I were positive it would come true." Grinning, she handed him the sign. "We'll not only have a place to live, you'll be able to stop paying rent on a separate office and we'll have plenty of extra money."

Laughing, he laid aside the sign and stood to embrace her. "When you get your mind set on something you don't give up, do you?"

"No, I don't. You should be delighted because that means I'm never going to stop loving you."

"And I will always be totally yours," Taylor vowed. "Set a date. We're getting married just as soon as we can."

Epilogue

Sara Beth had not asked her brothers to call her "Mama"; it had simply happened naturally after she and Taylor had had a son of their own.

Luke was currently apprenticed to a saddle maker in Benecia while Mathias continued his schooling back east. Josiah, now nearly ten, had no recollection of Isabella or Robert Reese, so the transition had been easiest on him.

"Mama, there's a man here who says you're needed," Josiah called from the front of the house.

Quickly removing her apron, Sara Beth hurried to the parlor and found a harried husband, pacing, hat in hand. "Is it time?" she asked him.

"Yes'm. She says so."

"Well, it's her fourth baby, so we have to assume

she knows," Sara Beth said. She turned to Josiah. "Watch your brother for me till your papa gets home, will you? He was making the circuit to Mission Dolores today, so he shouldn't be very late getting back. Supper's on the stove and there are cookies you can share if you get hungry before then."

"Yes, ma'am."

"And tell your father that he won't be needed unless I send for him." The look on the boy's face made her smile.

"I have been a midwife for longer than he had been a doctor when we met," she said. "My patients and I will be fine."

Swinging a shawl over her shoulders, she picked up a black bag that was identical in size and shape to the one Taylor carried. He never seemed to tire of telling her how much he admired her and her work. That, and having a chance to help other women, was enough for Sara Beth.

She smiled as she turned to the expectant father. "Let's be going. Babies don't wait for anything and I can hardly wait to greet your newest family member."

* * * * *

Dear Reader,

As I was researching this book I found an amazing number of disturbing facts about life in San Francisco in 1856–57. For the sake of carrying the story along I have compressed the outcome slightly. The results remain accurate. Naturally, the Reese family and Dr. Hayward are fictitious, but the background is all too real. If I had not read this history for myself I would not have believed it.

Sara Beth has the spirit of a pioneer and the heart of a loving Christian, yet she faces many hardships and dangers during the course of this book. That kind of difficulty is not unusual, as I have learned during my years as a believer. We may be saved for eternity, yes, but we still have to do the best we can with what we are given. I firmly believe that it is by finding God's peace amidst trials that we truly blossom and grow.

I love to hear from my readers. The easiest way to reach me is by e-mail, val@valeriehansen.com or send a letter to P.O. Box 13, Glencoe, AR 72539. You can also see my other work at valeriehansen.com.

Blessings,

Valerie Hansen

QUESTIONS FOR DISCUSSION

1. Did it seem unusual to you that Sara Beth would venture out at night? Why? Is she acting irresponsibly by taking her younger siblings along? What else could she have done?

2. Have you ever known and accepted someone as different from the mainstream as old Abe Warner is? How did you manage to get past first impressions?

3. Do you think that being a Christian helps people accept others, or can it be an additional reason to be overly critical? What did Jesus do?

4. Once her parents were deceased, Sara Beth sought out the orphanage for help for her family. Was there something else she could have done?

5. Dr. Taylor Hayward actually studied at a medical school. Had most doctors in that era done so? Why not?

6. When Sara Beth says she wants to become a doctor, too, Abe and others laugh at her. Why was this dream so laughable back then? Did a young woman have any other options? Why or why not?

7. Politics in nineteenth-century San Francisco were in turmoil. Now that we have become more aware of what is going on in the world, would it still be possible for the authorities to be so corrupt without being caught at it? Why or why not?

8. Were you surprised that there were so many newspapers in the city and that they were also very politically oriented?

9. When the Vigilance Committee took the law into its own hands, was it right or wrong, given the unfairness of the legal system? What would you have done?

10. Earthquakes were very common in San Francisco in the 1800s and still are today. Would you be afraid to live there, or would you just accept the shaking because it happened so often?

11. Sara Beth is worried that Taylor will not want to marry her because of her stepfather's tarnished reputation. Is that a fair assessment, or should she have given him the benefit of the doubt?

12. Why do you think she failed to ask him to be specific about his intentions? Was she afraid of what he might say?

13. When Taylor takes on Sara Beth's whole family, is he exceptional, or was that the norm in those days? What would you have done?

HISTORICAL

TITLES AVAILABLE NEXT MONTH

Available July 13, 2010

DAKOTA COWBOY
Linda Ford

THE PROTECTOR
Carla Capshaw

*Introducing McFARLANE'S PERFECT BRIDE
by* USA TODAY *bestselling author Christine Rimmer,
from Silhouette Special Edition®.*

Entranced. Captivated. Enchanted.

Connor sat across the table from Tori Jones and couldn't help thinking that those words exactly described what effect the small-town schoolteacher had on him. He might as well stop trying to tell himself he wasn't interested. He was powerfully drawn to her.

Clearly, he should have dated more when he was younger.

There had been a couple of other women since Jennifer had walked out on him. But he had never been entranced. Or captivated. Or enchanted.

Until now.

He wanted her—*her,* Tori Jones, in particular. Not just someone suitably attractive and well-bred, as Jennifer had been. Not just someone sophisticated, sexually exciting and discreet, which pretty much described the two women he'd dated after his marriage crashed and burned.

It came to him that he…he *liked* this woman. And that was new to him. He liked her quick wit, her wisdom and her big heart. He liked the passion in her voice when she talked about things she believed in.

He liked *her.* And suddenly it mattered all out of proportion that she might like him, too.

Was he losing it? He couldn't help but wonder. Was he cracking under the strain—of the soured economy, the McFarlane House setbacks, his divorce, the scary changes in his son? Of the changes he'd decided he needed to make in his life and himself?

Strangely, right then, on his first date with Tori Jones, he didn't care if he just might be going over the edge. He was having a great time—having *fun,* of all things—and he didn't want it to end.

Is Connor finally able to admit his feelings to Tori, and are they reciprocated?
Find out in McFARLANE'S PERFECT BRIDE
by USA TODAY bestselling author Christine Rimmer.
Available July 2010,
only from Silhouette Special Edition®.